In the Thick
of a
WHIPPOORWILL
Heart

SHARON MARIE BRASHER

For Betty Jo, the mother I needed. And for Dede, the mother I gained when I won the friendship lottery.

CHAPTER ONE

Maybe it's best you never know what lies in the thick of my heart,
its fathomless sorrows that run like rivers through.
So deep that at times, I am crushed under the pressure of what I know
and feel.
And if the expression of this pain is uncomfortable for you to hear, I
apologize to no one.

-The Whippoorwill

I remember the exact day I decided to open up an electronics repair shop. It was the same day my plan to go on to get my master's degree, to become a counselor specializing in working with traumatized children, was abruptly derailed.

It was late spring. The sun shined directly into my eyes as I hurried across the hospital campus, squinting at the pink blooms of dogwoods that seemed to appear suddenly around every corner.

I'd intended to arrive early, eager to complete my clinical course work, the only thing left for me to do to ensure that I graduated on time with my Bachelor of Science in

Psychology from the University of Tennessee. A wreck on the highway had laid waste to that and I was twenty minutes late when I breathlessly stormed into Dr. Willingham's office.

He was a native of NYC with a reputation for not having a filter. Rubbing him the wrong way left students open to being chewed a new asshole, and then some.

But instead of a strong reprimand for wasting his time, he took one look at me, adjusted his wire rimmed frames, and smiled, "Don't bother. I already know about the accident. Even my assistant hasn't made it in yet."

He stood, revealing his lanky frame, slid a couple of files inside of a chunky metal clip board, and closed its lid, "Shall we?"

I struggled to keep up with him, his brisk pace and impossibly long legs, forcing me to take on a sort of hybrid speed walk/jog. The contents of my book bag that included a Thermos of coffee and a container of fried chicken I'd snuck out of the dining hall the previous evening, clanged noisily, drawing embarrassing stares.

When we reached the psych ward, he motioned toward my bag, "Why don't you leave that here?"

My cheeks flushed crimson as I removed a notebook and pen and tucked it underneath the main desk.

For the rest of the morning, I was his shadow as he made his rounds. And it was there that I encountered a woman who reminded me of my mother.

She was frailer, more delicate, not blonde haired and grey eyed, or of good, solid German stock like her, but there was a glint in her eyes when she spotted me, an all-knowing demon dwelling inside that sensed everything she needed to know to poke at the wounds buried deep within.

Her hair had been wavy, the jet black made darker by the oils from her scalp that had slid quickly down to the ends of its shoulder length. There were fresh scabs on the side of her neck where she had dug her fingernails in. And for this, she had been strapped into the bed, with her own safety and the safety of hospital staff in mind.

I watched as the doctor interacted with her, but she was more focused on me, "Ahh...I get it. You think you're going to do this type of work. You don't have the stomach for it. You're weak, a weak little boy who runs away when the going gets tough. How does someone like yourself help someone like me? Do you see the problem?" she asked.

I smiled politely at her. "I'm sure I'll manage."

"Will you?"

The doctor was too experienced to let this type of banter throw him off course and immediately turned the focus back to his patient, "Elizabeth, you're being rude. Instead of spending so much time focused on the shortcomings of others, perhaps it would serve us better to focus on why you are in this room, in this bed."

The woman began to scream, a shrill and nerve-wracking tenor, reaching a decibel scale that such a small person should not have been able to achieve. And for the rest of our time in her hospital room, it did not let up.

It wasn't until later that evening, back in my dorm room, less than one month from graduation, that it dawned on me that the manic woman, Elizabeth, had posed a question I had not dared to.

It had struck a nerve, hit upon a fear that was hiding within my subconscious, unexplored. It was a feeling of foreboding that my life would become an endless stream of rooms like that, spending time with people, who like my own mother, had something intrinsically wrong in the core of their beings, something I might never be able to cure them of.

The thing inside of that patient was so like the thing inside of my own mother that had caused such pain and torment throughout my childhood and adolescence.

How could I be a savior for others when I couldn't find the courage to delve into dark recesses of my own mind and confront what was in there?

After I received my diploma, I used money I'd been saving to go toward furthering my education and opened up *Electronics Doctor*.

I was good at repair work. It had supported me through college. I liked the idea of creating a world for myself, one that I could control completely, down to what temperature I set the thermostat to, what color I painted the walls, what hours I would keep, what days I would open, who I let in, and who I didn't.

There was something deeply satisfying about taking something broken and bringing it back to life. I was the supreme keeper of the circuit board, replacer of lost bolts, and finder of obsolete parts.

This world I understood. It was governed purely by schematics. I could cure whatever ailed, as long as the right part existed. And this made me happy.

But 10 years later, the world had changed. My business had dwindled. Computers and sim cards, rendered much of what I did irrelevant. More and more, I found I could not fix the things that came through my door. And I myself was slowly but surely becoming a relic.

My girlfriend Sandy didn't seem to mind that I was headed in the opposite direction of millionairedom, or that I still lived in a large apartment above my shop. She didn't push me for commitment and was content with seeing me only once or twice a week.

This was not surprising given that Sandy was a divorce lawyer, severely jaded by everything she had witnessed. She'd seen the worst of the worst. She never wanted children. To her, marriage seemed like a surefire path to constant disappointment and restraining orders.

Sandy was so different from my 6'1, pale skin, and dirty blonde hair. She was petite, 5'3 in heels, and curvaceous. She was beautiful. I mean, drop dead gorgeous.

Her parents were from Costa Rica, and she had inherited pale golden-brown skin and glossy, dark brown hair that I loved to bury my hands in when we made love. Her eyes reminded me of fossilized amber.

When we were together, we only focused on each other. There was love and warmth. There were breakfasts in bed and true comradery. We were as close to perfect as a couple of people could hope to get.

I felt like the luckiest man on the planet to have her in my life.

But when we were apart, it was as if we lived on different planets, our worlds cut off and disconnected. We didn't text each other during the day or call just to say goodnight.

And this is the way it went, until she showed up once again with her overnight bag in hand, and it was as if no time at all had passed.

We didn't talk about the future or wonder what would become of us if either person demanded more, as if there was an unspoken understanding that neither of us ever would. It was inconceivable that anything would ever change.

The call came on a Wednesday afternoon. The woman's voice on the other end was laced with a pronounced Appalachian drawl. "I'm a nurse over at Piney Ridge Hospital and we have your name down as an emergency contact for Rita Winston. We've been trying to get in touch with you. I left a message. Did you get it?"

I felt the rush of adrenaline, a familiar stress response upon hearing my mother's name. "I may have listened to part of the message. I deleted it as soon as I realized who you were calling about. I'm not sure how I can help you. I haven't spoken to her in nearly twenty years."

"Oh, I see." There was an awkward pause. "It's just that…she doesn't have anybody else. A neighbor found her and let's just say that her living conditions were pretty horrific. Clearly, she will not able to live on her own anymore."

"Listen, I really wish I could help you, but my mother has done this to herself."

As if sensing that I was on the verge of hanging up, the nurse spoke more frankly, "Mr. Winston, your mother has end-stage Alzheimer's disease. She has severe COPD aggravated by her unwillingness to stop smoking. She had an infection from the neuropathy in her right leg that was so severe they had to amputate her foot when they brought her in. The doctors weren't even sure that she would survive the surgery, but she has."

I clenched the phone in stunned silence. All these years I'd done a pretty excellent job of forgetting that she even existed, or that she still lived less than an hour away. But hearing the nurse say those words pulled at my emotions in a way I had not anticipated.

But what was it that I was feeling? Relief? Sadness? Anger?

That was hard to say.

"Are you still there?" she asked.

"I'm here," I said weakly, but nothing else came.

My pulse raced and I felt a throbbing pressure in my head. The nurse filled in this silence with more details about Rita's condition.

But when she asked if I could please come there and speak with her face to face, I made an impulsive decision, "I'll be there in an hour."

There was relief in the woman's voice. "Thank you. I'll be waiting. Just come to the fourth-floor and ask for Denise."

I turned all the lights out, flipped the sign on the storefront to closed, and locked up. The furnace of July heat rose up from the asphalt as much of an assault to my senses as the phone call had been.

Behind the steering wheel of my white Bronco, I was aware of an acute sense of dread. And I was sure the sweat dripping off of my forehead was from anxiety, not heat.

My thoughts slipped back to the day I'd graduated from high school, the day I had decided to cut my mother off forever.

Like my fellow classmates, I had been excited about the future. Unlike them, I hadn't been flush with cash from checks rolling in from distant relatives. We hadn't had anyone.

It had just been me and Mamma, my only living relative and the person I wanted most to escape from.

With a scholarship to the University of Tennessee lined up and a job waiting for me in Knoxville, this was going to be possible.

I had thrown my cap into the air that afternoon and driven home. There had been no cake to celebrate this milestone, no streaming ribbons tied to balloons in my school colors of red and white, waiting for me.

Instead, I had found my mother passed out drunk on the couch next to shards of a whiskey bottle that had likely slipped from her hand and shattered on the floor.

If there had been anything festive about that day, it had been the years of pent-up emotions that exploded from me like a can of silly string gone dangerously berserk, "Lazy, selfish, piece of shit. You don't care about anyone! Why can't you care about anyone besides yourself?"

My mother had winced and opened her eyes, "What are you bellowing about? Because I don't give a shit about some worthless diploma? Why would I care about that, Halby?"

She'd rolled over, turning her back to me, and in no time at all, was snoring again.

For a long time, I had stood there watching. I waited for the pain to ebb away and for the numbness to take its place the way it always did.

Her pouty lips and the way she had curled into a semi-fetal position with her finger curled around a strand of her hair, made her look innocent. It had almost been endearing.

A clueless observer might have thought that she looked sweet, that something good and pure still remained inside of her.

But I'd been fooled by that before. Enough times to know the truth. There was nothing good left inside of my mother.

I had left a note, which was already way more effort than she would have gone to for me. It had been short and to the point.

Fuck off! May I never have to see your fucking face again.

When I'd left that day, I had no place to go and a full summer ahead of me. I'd always wanted to go to Florida. Why not?

After I'd packed up my few belongings and bought a map. I had marked a random place with a red felt tip pen. Pensacola. And then I'd filled up my tank with gas.

Something had happened to me there, with my toes dug into the sand, with the waves lapping over me while the dragonflies whizzed about.

I had watched the boats sailing in the far distance and Navy planes flying overhead, and had understood that life was not all shit and muck.

Being completely alone with myself, had allowed me to believe that there was more to life than cortisol surges or being hit in the face by a metal bowl hurled at 30 miles an hour.

There hadn't been anybody around telling me how useless I was. I had understood that I was free to make my life whatever I wanted it to be.

After a summer spent sleeping in my car, living off the money I'd made working at the dingy dive of botulism known as *Dan's Burgers*, eating ramen noodles cooked to boiling on the dash of my car, and depending on the charity of friends and strangers, I had been reborn.

I'd buried my past, the same way I'd buried my feet in the sand. I had become an orphan, the only person I ever needed to count on and that had given me intense peace.

Going forward, I would avoid overly, dramatic people. I would keep my world small.

I would never let anybody hurt me again.

CHAPTER TWO

I pulled into the parking lot of Piney Ridge Hospital, the only hospital in the community of Piney View. It was a small regional facility that I remembered as being a place of last resort, where you went when you were either too poor or too sick to make it to UT Medical Center.

The dilapidated building I'd known as a child had been renovated into a shiny new one. It dawned on me that there used to be only two floors to this hospital and that they had added on two more.

I glanced up toward the place where my mother lay in wait, probably sharpening her fingernails in hopes of a chance to gouge out my eyes for being such an asshole to her.

When I stepped off the elevator, I was met with a locked door and a reception window. It was obvious that this was the designated psychiatric floor.

An attractive, older, African American woman glared at me with eyebrows lifted, as if waiting for me to realize that I was in the wrong place.

When I didn't immediately, high tail it out of there, she pointed at the wall where there was an intercom and a sign to indicate she couldn't hear me unless I hit the button.

"I'm Hal Winston. I'm here to see Denise."

She smiled sweetly, her voice slightly crackling as it was distorted by the speaker, "I will let her know you're here. I will need to get a copy of your driver's license," she said.

A drawer sprang open long enough for me to place my ID inside. I watched her make a copy of it and return it through the drawer.

She motioned to a row of uncomfortable looking faux leather chairs. "Denise will be out to get you shortly."

A few minutes later the door opened and Denise Atchley appeared. I assessed that she was in her late forties. I wondered if her personality was as spicey as her hair, almost unnaturally red, cut into an angular, chin length bob with thick bangs.

She directed me into a small closet of an office. "I'm so relieved you came. Would you like a coffee or something to drink?"

"No, I'm good, but thanks. Like I said on the phone, I'm not sure what I can do for you."

"In cases such as these with no family member willing to care for her, a decision will have to be made about a facility."

"Sounds like you've got this all under control."

"It's just that with the Alzheimer's and her combative nature, we are looking at her being restrained in some capacity for the majority of her last days on this earth. I just didn't want to see that happen if another solution could be worked out." I could see Denise was still hoping that

13

knowing more about the reality of my mother's situation would soften me up.

"Sorry for not having a whole lot of sympathy for the mother who physically battered and emotionally abused me for the first eighteen years of my life."

Denise nodded and I could see in her eyes that this did not surprise her. She already suspected this.

"Your mother has said some truly hateful and mean things to our staff. There is a lot of unflattering information in her file too, years and years of it. She's been fired by more doctors than I care to recount because of her abusive behavior."

Denise leaned forward and clasped her hands on top of my mother's file. "She has probably had this disease for a very long time, but it's been hidden by her alcoholism. She is a very sick woman." She took her reading glasses off and laid them to the side of her desk. "But there have been days this week when I have walked in there and she is just as sweet as jam on toast and I could only love her for it. She's grown on me. And I suppose, I just want to make sure I've done everything that I can possibly do to help her."

"My mother? Sweet?"

"Well… not this morning she wasn't. She got a hold of one of the aides and nearly pulled her bald headed. We've since adjusted her medication. Her sweetness sort of comes in waves."

That sounded more like the woman I knew, minus the sweet part. That narcissistic woman would chew off her right arm before showing anyone kindness.

14

I'd always wondered how someone as salty as she was, could even make a living as a waitress. I figured she'd lasted at Wyley's Diner all those years because she had some kind of dirt to hold over the owner's head. That or Martin Wyley was afraid that she would break into his house and suffocate him in his sleep.

But there was something very unsettling about being told she was in her last days, that the only person I was related to and had blamed for the most miserable childhood imaginable, would in a short time, no longer be walking among the living.

"How long does she have?" I asked.

"It's hard to say. Days. Weeks. Only the man above knows that."

"Alright. I'll see her. I should at least say goodbye." I could hear the lyrics to an old tune playing in my head, *so long, it's been good to know yuh*.

But it hadn't been good. Not ever. There were no happy memories to bind us together and that would live on. All that we had were the unpleasant shadows of things I'd done my best to forget.

That was our legacy, our last vestige of home.

Nurse Denise smiled then. I could see the relief in her face that she had been able to broker this bridge between us. But there was something else to it, a glint in her eyes, and I had to convince myself that there was nothing smug and self-satisfied lurking in it.

I followed her down a long hallway to a room that held a woman I did not recognize. My mother had always been tall, 5'11", and sturdy. This person was a thin, frail wraith, pale skin with tributaries of visible blue veins branching out.

Gone were her golden locks, now it was long and fine, almost the same color as the stark white of the pillow case. With her eyes shut, she took in quick, shallow breaths, through her oxygen mask.

Her arms were bound in a straitjacket because of the incident earlier in the day, though she hardly seemed capable of lifting a cereal box, let alone, inflicting injury upon anyone.

She looked vulnerable. And of all of the images I held in my mind of what I would find. This was not one of them.

As if reading my mind, the nurse spoke softly, mindful that her patient could likely hear every word. "She has a lot of fight left in her, strength that comes in from who knows where, and she rallies and tries to get out of that bed. But then there are times like now."

Like now, meaning when she looked like she was knock-knock-knocking on heaven or hell's door. In all honesty, we could not really be certain which one would be available when the time came, now could we?

Emotions rushed in, and it felt like a bundle of steel wool had collected in my throat. I did not know this person.

For an instant, I considered that it was all a huge mistake, that they had mixed up the patients and this was not my mother at all. But the small, delicate scar in the center of her forehead, just below her hairline and its distinct starburst shape, left no doubt.

As if sensing the emotional charge in the room, Rita Winston opened her bluish grey eyes. She let them settle on me for several seconds before recognition set in.

I held my breath, waiting for the cruel onslaught that only years of stewing rage could foster. But then a flash of light registered inside of them and a tear rolled down her cheeks.

"Halby...is it you?"

I had not been prepared for this. Somehow, I found my voice, choking out, "It's me, Mamma."

I braced for the sledgehammer of words that always pulverized anything beautiful, any moment that made me feel connected to her, into dust.

She only smiled and said, "I'm so happy you came. I'd like to go home now. Can you take me home?" And immediately, slipped back into a very deep sleep.

With my mother's keys that I'd obtained from Denise in hand, I drove to the family home on Gilbert Street, the place I'd always lived with my mother.

It had been handed down to her from her mother, Ingrate Winston, who had inherited it from her parents, Parker and Elise Winston.

Parker had purchased the kit for the Craftsman style home from a Sears Roebuck Catalogue, which contained everything needed, including the nails, to erect the frame. But now it was in bad shape, the eaves were full of rot, and the paint peeled away.

Ingrate, passed away when I was only a baby. There was a lot of mystery surrounding my mother's father. I knew that his name was Norman and that he had been a good for nothing slacker who liked to booze it up. And that he had hastily gone his own way one sunny May afternoon never to be seen or heard from again.

I planted my foot on the bottom step of the front porch, only to have a brick break away and send me stumbling backward. I wondered how close to the edge of collapse it was. But upon closer inspection, other than the loose brick and wobbly railing, it was pretty solid.

When the door was opened, the smell sent me fleeing back into the yard. I decided another strategy was needed and waded through tall grass and weeds toward the back entrance.

Careful this time to hold my breath, I opened the kitchen door wide. I lingered at the threshold for a good 10 minutes while a cross breeze swept out some of the odor of rot and I processed what I saw inside.

Once inside, I was confronted with counters that had long ago disappeared beneath heaps of empty containers. Ice cream cartons and frozen dinner trays writhed with maggots. It was hard to fathom what sort of filth was smeared onto the walls.

I assumed that the wet sticky grime that glued multi-colored candy wrappers to a bog-like floor, was the result of a leaking roof. This was not surprising considering how much that section of the ceiling sagged.

My first instinct was to strike a match and burn it all to the ground. And it was extremely difficult to suppress that urge. But then something macabre took hold of me and I walked slowly through every room, taking in the complete state of disrepair, the collateral damage left behind by a brain gone completely haywire.

When I reached my mother's bedroom, I gagged at the strong stench of urine and had to pull my shirt up to cover my nose and mouth.

The light wouldn't switch on, likely a blown bulb. I struggled to make my way through total darkness, nailing the corner of a coffee table, sitting oddly in the middle of the room, with my knee cap, "For the love of Pete!"

I pulled open the blackout curtains and struggled with the window until it budged some. It was enough to allow a hot breeze to penetrate the heavy foulness and to take in what daylight revealed.

To my complete horror, I realized that the uneven clumps of brown, splattered against every surface like a monochromatic art project carried out by emo monkeys, was dried feces.

Nurse Denise had said that when they found her, she'd lost too much strength in her legs to walk. Mainly, this had resulted from the infection in her foot that had prevented her from putting pressure on it for a long period of time.

She had been hanging on to life by the thinnest thread. The only reason they had showed up at all was because a neighbor had called the police and expressed concern about her well-being.

Otherwise, the phone call I'd received might have been quite different.

I wondered if that would have been a blessing, instead of being here, faced with the dilemma of what to do with her.

Then I felt guilty for even having that thought.

Then I felt sad because she was the woman who brought me into this world and she was obviously, very ill, and I knew this and still had this thought.

I'd convinced myself that the past had been forgotten, that it was no longer a part of me. What I hadn't realized up until this moment, was that what I'd really been doing all these years leading up to the now, was building an illusion around myself.

I'd been hanging the proverbial sheetrock of my life, hiding within these walls while ignoring the wounds that were still festering behind them.

Maybe the powers above had given me signs, I don't know.

Maybe I ignored the subtle promptings trying to shake me out of my denial.

Maybe this was the reason that the universe had decided it was time to really get my attention by strategically blasting a 5/16 combination wrench into one of these walls.

On its own, it was a tiny little fucker, but enough to destabilize the load bearing integrity and expose all the fire hazards these erupting pustules posed to the wiring that made up *me*.

I had a knowing about this situation with my mother, that it was designed to do this. And it was my choice to decide what I would do about it.

What was the right thing to do?

When my mother had been in control of herself, it had been easy to blame her, cut her off, and eradicate her from my life. Now, I felt obligated in spite of my resentments around her.

Looking back, would I be OK with doing nothing?

Or would I regret not doing all I could to make her transition easier?

And what was to be done about the state of this house? About anything?

It was difficult to imagine her trapped in here alone, but to think of anyone dying like this, with no one around who cared about them. It tore me up inside.

Nobody deserved their last days on earth to be like this. Nobody. Not even her.

The bedside table had been knocked over. Its items were strewn across the floor, a broken ceramic lamp, a cordless telephone tipped off of its cradle, and a picture frame. But there wasn't a picture inside of it.

I recognized it instantly. It was the savage note I'd left behind for her.

The old croon had framed it!

I laughed out loud. It was so Rita Winston to have done something like this.

Had it been in there all these years, collecting dust, reminding her of what a worthless son I was? Or was it there to stop her from reaching out to me in times of weakness?

I didn't feel good about either of those scenarios.

I'd passed a small Dollar Master store on my way in, the closest place I knew that would have cleaning supplies. I decided to take a different route back to it, driving through what was left of the downtown.

The main drag once thrived with businesses, but all that remained now were mostly shuttered buildings. Their solid brick, Art Deco architecture was still beautiful, even after a human lifetime of neglect.

Not like the gaudy metal buildings that sprang up around them, filled with paycheck lending sites, fast food chains, and all of the usual things impoverished towns possessed.

There weren't many well-paying jobs left in Piney View anymore. People had to drive the 45 minutes to Knoxville for that.

I found a parking spot close to the front of the store, and once inside, wandered aimlessly from aisle to aisle. I was still reeling from the thoughts stirring around inside of my head.

As if by their own volition pairs of rubber gloves, gallons upon gallons of bleach and cleaning fluids, scrubbing brushes, boxes of heavy-duty trash bags, and things I didn't even remember selecting, made their way inside my shopping cart.

They formed a menacing tower that threatened to come tumbling down with slightest provocation.

It was only after passing other shoppers and seeing the strange looks being cast my way, that I realized these were the very same items a person on their way to clean up a crime scene would purchase.

I merged into the line, smiling too widely at the gentleman in front of me. He did a double take, looked away quickly, then resorted to a curious, side-eye perusal of my cart.

When I reached the register, I couldn't resist asking the young cashier, "You don't sell large metal drums or acid here, do you?"

I heard a gasp from someone holding up the rear of the line.

The cashier was barely a teenager and stared back at me with her huge doe eyes, "No, sir. We don't have nuthin' like that."

I nodded, making sure to look extremely disappointed.

"That will be $97.57," she said nervously.

I handed her a $100 bill and winked as if we had a secret understanding between us, "Why don't you just keep the change."

She called after me, "Sir, I can't keep this! It's against the rules to accept tips."

I winked as I exited through the automatic doors, "I won't tell anyone if you don't."

A heavy-set woman, who seemed to be compensating for her diminutive height with big, teased up hair, and who was about as subtle as a big foot driving a Subaru, followed me out, pretending to sift through a sale bin on the sidewalk.

But her phone was aimed in my direction. I was pretty sure she was filming me the entire time I loaded up my vehicle.

I made sure to punch the gas hard enough for my tires to squeal out of the parking lot. But back at my mother's house all the humor faded away.

I let out a long, disgusted sigh at the task waiting for me. It was daunting and I didn't even know how or where I should start.

It took time to psyche myself up for it, but then I tied a bandana over my face and dug in, dragging bags of garbage to the curb and anything that I deemed unsalvageable.

I ripped up old towels to use, scrubbed away at feces that fell from the wall taking sections of plaster with it, and disinfected everything with massive amounts of bleach.

There was a point where I was no longer horrified by the process. It was something that had to be done, a task that I needed to get through.

Hours slipped by. At 3:00 am, I took a break and sat on the front stoop staring through the darkness.

I remembered all the nooks and crannies of the neighborhood, all the places that I used to hide when I didn't want to come home or when my mother decided she wanted to lock me out of the house all night.

I knew the porch directly across the street had a loose board on the side that had pivoted up just enough to allow me to slip underneath. I wondered if there were still remnants of the green, Army issued blanket that I'd bought at a thrift store for .50 cents or the disintegrating remains of graphic novels I'd abandoned there.

But my favorite spot had been an old tree house behind a rental property down the street. When the house was vacant or without tenants, which was most of the time, I holed up there. I did this mostly in the summertime when it was just me, the birds, the squirrels, and the cicadas.

One day, I'd asked a neighbor lady, Mrs. Hale, likely no longer among the living as she was older that the pyramids even back then, why she thought nobody ever lived in that house for long.

"There is speculation that the house is haunted. But who really knows? Maybe it's just the power of suggestion, playing tricks on people's minds."

I had never been inside of that house but I knew I'd never felt anything bad outside in the treehouse. There, I'd only felt safe. I'd prayed all summer that nobody would move in so that I could just keep hanging out there forever.

"Do you believe in ghosts, Mrs. Hale?"

She had laughed. "I most certainly, do. I've seen one, you know. In Savannah, while walking through the town square. A union soldier came rushing by me and disappeared right into thin air."

I wasn't sure if she had just been pulling my leg that day, telling a tale to entertain a young boy. But I started thinking about how me and that ghost must have had a special affinity.

We hadn't seemed to mind each other's company. Both of us, had wanted to have that space all for ourselves. We had wanted it to be peaceful and quiet, a place to anchor us and stop us from spinning out into the unknown.

Shuffling to the end of the driveway, I stood with my hands in the pockets of my faded Levi's and glanced down the street.

All evidence of that treehouse had been cleared away. It was long gone. A tall wooden privacy fence had been installed around the yard.

Someone had put some love into that house, though, painting it Kelly green and adding black storm shutters. It looked like a permanent home.

Pale yellow light swelled inside its windows, beckoning to me. I wondered who would still be awake at three in the morning and about what kind of person felt at home in a haunted house?

I checked my phone. I knew Sandy had tried to call me. This was probably because she had showed up and been surprised that I hadn't been there waiting for her, the way I always had been.

It was funny to think that in all this time, that had never happened before.

Everything about this day had a surreal quality, an, *I can't believe I'm here doing what I'm doing,* quality. Something, somewhere had shifted. And there was a feeling that went with it that I couldn't explain, that nothing in my life would ever be the same again.

I didn't bother to call Sandy back. I didn't know what to say, how to explain what had happened, or why I was doing what I was doing. It made more sense to get back to work, to finish everything that still needed to be done.

I had saved the worst part for last. Four hours later, I flipped my mother's mattress on its side. The liquid trapped within began to dribble out onto the hardwood floor.

The miasma that I'd stirred up, of ammonia mixed with the stink of fecal matter, was almost too much. I could feel vomit rising to the back of my throat and sought refuge in the now spotless bathroom, where I hung my head outside the window.

You can do this, Hal. Then you are free to go home and scrub all evidence of this horror show off of you.

I made a tarp out of duct tape and plastic bags and wrapped them around the mattress. That way I could get it through the front door without ruining the floors I'd already cleaned. Then I unceremoniously, deposited it in the middle of the front yard.

Bright sunlight wreaked havoc on my sleep deprived eyes. I hadn't noticed that I was not alone until I heard the scream that erupted behind me, nearly scaring the ever-loving hell out of me.

"Sweet, baby Jesus! Was somebody murdered on that?"

As fate would command, it was the same woman from the store, only she was without her cell phone this time.

She wore curlers in her hair, a blue fuzzy bathrobe, and held a leash that was attached to the tiniest chihuahua I'd ever seen.

It barked aggressively, baring itty, bitty teeth, ready to sink them into me. I figured it might at least be able to reach my ankles and break the skin.

Her anxiety and the pitch of her screams only seemed to grow more frantic when she realized I was the maniac she'd taken pictures of the evening before.

She picked up her dog, protectively, and backed away, "What have you done with Ms. Winston?"

For shits and giggles, I took a step toward her and held out my yellow, latex covered hand, "Why, good morning. It's a fine, fine day. A good day for a fire, wouldn't you say?"

Even though there was a good fifteen feet between us, she swatted at the air around her as if keeping a swarm of African bees at bay. This would have done hardly, any good at all had I actually been a psychotic killer. "You stay away from me. I'm calling the police."

Then she ran away as fast as her stubby little legs would carry her. I watched her depart with a sort of dark delight percolating inside of me.

I threw all of the dirty sheets, cleaning rags, and the box springs on top of the mattress, doused them with old gasoline I'd found in the shed, and set them on fire.

The flames rose up with billowing black smoke, hissing from all of the moisture inside. It was larger than I had expected, an impressive and satisfying bonfire that raged as I waited for the police to come.

CHAPTER THREE

When the patrol car pulled into the driveway, I made no effort to budge from where I leaned against the mostly rusted, porch railing, drinking an ice-cold cola.

The officer had a stereo-typical look about him. He was middle aged, Caucasian, and slow moving, a true Southerner with a perpetually bored expression and an irritable disposition.

He was clearly the result of a Piney View High diploma and what happened when a person never left the bubble of a small town.

This wasn't so much a judgement as a simple observation. I mean, I too held that same diploma and without my scholarship to UT, who knows? I might have ended up wearing that same uniform, equally as crotchety.

With a surprisingly, unhurried saunter, he made his way to me. It was surprising because I was sure by this point, he'd heard the whole story about how a serial killer had murdered Rita Winston and was now destroying evidence in full view of the entire neighborhood.

"I'm Officer Kubrick. We had a complaint about a possible crime at this address," he said.

"Is it a crime to burn a mattress on the front lawn?"

"As a matter of fact, it is. You can't just go about burning who know what kind of toxic crap without a burn permit."

"Well then…I guess it's a good thing you came to stop me, although you might be a tad late. Are you going to arrest me, Officer?" I was sure the man detected my thinly veiled sarcasm.

He grimaced, "Son, you smell like shit."

With so many hours spent wading through festering garbage, it was inevitable that my hair and clothing would soak all of that goodness right up too.

"Yes sir, I suppose I do," I said, as if no other explanation were needed.

"Who the hell are you?" he asked.

"I'm Rita Winston's son, Hal."

He took his time looking me and the scene that was unfolding, over. Without a word he headed back to his patrol car and picked up his radio. Muffled voices, the sound of static, and he was back.

"So here is the deal…I'm going to overlook this incident. I realize your mother is very ill and if it were up to me this house would be condemned. It might have been a better idea to burn *it* to the ground."

"I did consider that, Officer."

He threw his hands into the air. "Why did you go and tell me that? You do know that is arson, right?"

"Why did you tell me it was a good idea?"

"It was a *joke!*" His exasperated tone rose a full octave on the word, joke.

But I said nothing in reply because I really had considered putting this old house out of its misery.

"I think we got off on the wrong foot. Your mother has been more than a little touched in the head for a few years now. I mean that in the kindest way possible. I've been to this address more times than I can count because she has been a nightmare, calling the police on just about everyone who lives on this street."

"What for?" I asked.

There was a morbid curiosity behind the question. The mother I knew went to work as a waitress five days a week, and spent all of her off time boozed to oblivion.

She had never put forth the effort to actually deal with any of the people she considered to be out to get her. Let's face it. She thought everyone in the world was against her.

But I knew it was more complicated than having too much time on her hands since receiving her social security. Her dementia had swooped in and completely changed the game. And I wanted to know all the details of this new version of my mother.

Officer Kubrick pulled out a pocket notebook and began to read from one of its pages, "On Christmas day of last year, she called us to report that the neighbors across the street had stolen her Christmas turkey out of the fridge, but it turns out they were visiting with family in Cleveland, Ohio, at the time, and oh yeah, she had never actually purchased a turkey. She remembered this detail in the midst of me writing out a report. In January, she called us to see how she could get a restraining order against another neighbor because she believed the woman was a witch who had been casting spells on her."

He paused long enough to assess my reaction. When he only encountered raised eyebrows, he read on. "Oh, and in February she ran the witch neighbor down with riding a lawn mower she had stolen from another neighbor's garage. Luckily, she only managed to run over her own mailbox. Neither of those neighbors pressed charges because they felt sorry for her. What I would like to know is where the hell have you been all this time?"

"Knoxville, Tennessee, Sir."

He looked shocked by my answer. I could see him sorting through his own ideas about family connection and loyalty, feelings about his mother and the love he had for her.

I knew he would never be able to understand the dynamic that had kept me away all of these years. He'd already made up his mind about me, that I was the worst kind of no-good son who ever lived.

"Which concerned neighbor called for the wellness check on my mother?"

"Believe it or not, it was the witch lady, Molly Owens."

"And where does this Molly person live?"

"In the bright green house, #222," he said. "I'll get out of your hair. Clean this crap up, or I will issue you a citation. And for Lord's sake, stop scaring the neighbors."

I watched the patrol car back away as I gulped down the last of my cola, hoping the caffeine would give me the pick me up I needed to keep from crashing.

I waited for the fire to die down before I went back inside. The only room I hadn't touched was my old bedroom. It had probably been turned into a storage heap by now. I cracked the door and peered in, surprised to find everything was in order and spotless.

It looked almost the same way it had the last time I'd seen it, and for reasons I couldn't explain, this disturbed me much more than anything else had.

I closed the door without venturing inside.

Hours later, the house reeked of bleach. I lit the vanilla candles I'd purchased at the Dollar Master and left them to do their magic while I climbed onto the roof with a blue tarp I'd taken out of my Bronco.

I inspected the leaking section. It was bad, with rotted boards that would have to be replaced. I secured the tarp as best as I could, the only temporary fix I had at my disposal. The damage was extensive and would not be cheap to repair.

When all the embers had cooled, I raked up the remaining debris and tossed it into one of the heavy-duty garbage bags. When I was done, a huge charred rectangle on the ground was all that remained.

It was five p.m., more than 24 hours from the time I'd stood by my mother's bedside, almost 28 hours since I'd last eaten anything.

I locked everything up and passed by the only green house on the street, #222. It was the haunted house.

Was that why my mother had gotten it into her head that the neighbor was a witch?

In the daylight I could make out the vibrant red of the roses that grew up a trellis next to the front window and a flower bed full of daylilies. Just looking at that house with all its new curb appeal and charm, filled me up with joy.

Maybe there was some ancient art like Feng Shui at work in provoking this feeling or it was pure happiness that someone had grown to love it as much as I had.

Or was my mother actually on the mark? Did a witch really live there? A witch with a green thumb. A witch with a heart of gold.

I-40 was heavy with traffic, but I hardly noticed it, or that it took me over an hour to get back home. I felt numb, unbothered by the aggressive drivers jockeying to get a few feet ahead of me and everyone else.

I had more serious things on my mind. An idea was beginning to take form.

I didn't bother to take down the sign I'd hung on the door the day before. I threw the clothes I'd been wearing out the window, easily clearing the dumpster in the back alley, and spent half an hour in the shower.

I contemplated calling Sandy back. She'd left so many voice and text messages that I'd been too overwhelmed to even listen to or read them all.

Instead, I made an egg sandwich and a pot of coffee, and went through my log book of items awaiting repair. There weren't many things to do. I had all the parts in stock. I could delay sleep for two more hours and get them done.

After midnight, I sent out emails to all of my clients.

35

Dear Customer,

I have completed the repair you submitted for service. Due to a family emergency, my presence is needed elsewhere. I would be happy to deliver your items directly to you at some time today. If we are unable to make arrangements, I have no idea when I will be available again. Please advise.

Sincerely,

Hal Winston

It was time to get some sleep, before I began to have Hunter S. Thompson inspired hallucinations that involved melting walls and giant weeping birds. *Why are you doing this, Hal? Just stay here with us, where it's safe,* they would say.

Because the hallucinations would already know my deepest, darkest thoughts, that I had made a guilt-ridden decision about what to do about my mother. And it was too late to change my mind.

CHAPTER FOUR

Nurse Denise held a gyro wrap in one hand when she waved me through. "Sorry, we are short staffed and I'm trying to grab a bite while I can."

"That's quite alright with me. Eat away."

She motioned toward a coffee pot and a basket of snack cakes and crackers, "Please, help yourself. I poured what looked like strong black coffee into a Styrofoam cup and sat in the same chair as before.

"Thank you. You said you didn't have a preference for a hospice company, so I contacted Tranquility Hospice on your behalf to get the ball running."

Tranquility, the name was duplicitous, sounding like a beach resort or a cruise ship name.

Was death tranquil?

I couldn't help but ponder this.

Denise continued, "A hospital bed has been requested, and they will deliver it to your mother's home, along with the oxygen machine. Will you be able to meet them there to receive these deliveries in five days?"

"Yes. I will. And you said the hospice team will provide a nurse for us?" I asked.

"Oh yes, of course. A nurse and someone to come and bathe your mother."

"What I'm committing to is foolish. Don't you think? I mean, I'm not a caregiver. I have no experience with this sort of thing." I waited for her to tell me that I was right and that I should abandon this idea immediately because she didn't see how this could possibly work out.

"No. I'd say many families are having to do what you are doing. Many because this is a much better option than the limited choices that are presented to them. Your mother paid into a retirement fund for a long time. She also receives a payment from a trust of some kind, and she owns a house that could be sold to pay for a facility if you decide that is the route you need to take. But with her unpredictable and violent outbursts, we already know what even being in a private facility will mean for her quality of life."

"That's surprising. I mean, I don't know anything about a trust. It could be something my late grandmother set up for her."

My great grandfather Parker, had been a pillar of the community, he owned property that he eventually sold. But business tycoon, he was not. I was sure that money ran out long ago.

"I am not sure of the details surrounding it." Denise took a bite of her wrap and flipped through some paperwork. "I see you have durable power of attorney that was granted back when you were 19 years-old."

"Really? Can I see that?"

"It was right before she had her right breast removed and then began a round of chemo." She handed over the document and I stared at my signature next to that of my mother's.

And then I remembered.

A letter and this document had arrived at my dorm at UT. My mother was having surgery and had wanted it in place in case something happened to her and she couldn't make decisions for herself.

At the time I hadn't given a good fuck. I had assumed she was having something minor done. I never wrote her back or called her about it. But I had taken the documents to a bank, signed them in front of a notary, and had the bank mail them back to the attorney for me.

I wondered who had been there with her while she went through this. Why hadn't she reached out? And if she had, would it have made a difference? I wasn't sure.

"I had forgotten all about this," I said.

"It's fortunate that this is in place. Especially, with all the hurdles we have to navigate these days with HIPAA. Dementia complicates things. There can be no question about her mental state when this was signed."

We both knew good and well that my mother's mental state had not been all that peachy, even back then, but we let this illusion stand.

Denise laid out several forms on the desk and went over my mother's follow-up care and medication schedule very slowly, before asking if I had any questions.

She saw my overwhelmed expression and said, "Don't worry. The nurse will be able to answer any questions that might come up later. Sign here."

"How is she today?" I asked as I signed next to the lopsided x.

"She has been sleeping all day. But they took her restraints off last night. I think we are all done here if you would like to check on her." Denise crammed the last bite of gyro into her mouth and licked tzatziki sauce off of her fingers. Then she cleaned them with a napkin, following up with hand sanitizer.

"Yes. Thank you. I'm hoping I can get everything fixed and ready in that time. Her house was in pretty bad shape."

"I did see there was a mention of that in the intake report. I have no doubt that you will be able to pull that off without a hitch. The staff at Tranquility Hospice will be in touch with you so keep your cell phone handy. If I don't see you again, Hal, good luck with everything. Bless you for doing this."

I only nodded. This wasn't some grand gesture. I was facilitating my mother's death, allowing her to return to her family home to die. And I didn't need a pat on the back for doing what felt like the right thing, especially, when I knew how miserably I could fail at it.

If my mother had been in her right mind, she would have informed Nurse Denise of how little faith she had in me and that I was most assuredly going to royally screw this up.

I observed Mamma's sleeping form from the doorway. Her head was tilted down against her pillow, drawn toward her left side just as she had been before, her lips pouting innocently.

"Mamma, it's Hal." When she didn't stir, I moved inside and touched her hand. Realizing it was ice cold, I pulled the cover up over it.

I couldn't recall a time when she had ever looked this frail. Had I ever seen her cry? Had she ever shown me tenderness or hugged me with a spontaneous outpouring of love?

Why did I only remember the hardness of this woman? Why could I not recall any soft and yielding moments? They must have existed somewhere, folded up within the hellscape of suffering that had gouged out our lives.

"I'm going to get you out of this place. I'm going to take you home."

She hadn't stirred, but I was sure that her breathing slowed, falling into a more peaceful rhythm as if she'd understood me.

I feared that she might be too weak to make the trip home, that she would die on the stretcher in the ambulance, not in her own room.

"Hang on just a little longer, Mamma."

Coming out of the deep freezer of the hospital, I welcomed the 90-degree heat and sweltering humidity as the ice crystals that had begun to form in my limbs, started to thaw.

41

My phone rang. It was Sandy. I had never called her back.

"Hey there, Sunshine."

"What the fuck, Hal. I was getting ready to file a missing person's report."

"I'm really sorry. I didn't mean to worry you. I'm in Piney View. My mother is sick."

"And you didn't have a minute to let me know that you weren't dead in a ditch somewhere. I thought you might have had a heart attack or something." I had never heard her sound this shrill and desperate.

"Heart attack? Jesus, Sandy, I know I'm a little older than you, but hopefully not old enough for hardened arteries."

She didn't appreciate my attempt at humor. "You have no idea of how thoroughly pissed off I am right now. Wait, didn't your mother push you out of a moving car when you were 13 because you got her menthol cigarettes by mistake? Why are you even there?"

"They called me. And she has nobody else. She's dying, Sandy."

"I'm sorry for not being particularly sympathetic but considering all that I know about her, I'm not sure if that is possible. How long do you think you will be there?"

"I don't know. She's being released into hospice care in five days."

"Would you like me to come, to be there for you?" There was reluctance in her tone, as if she were holding her breath, dreading me saying, yes.

Neither of us had ever stepped into a supporting role before and it was nobody's fault that we had no idea how to do it.

I cleared my throat, "No. Thank you for your offer. But I'm alright."

I could feel her relief. I hadn't really wanted her here with me, holding my hand, but the fact that she hadn't insisted, stood out, maybe even stung a little.

"I've arranged to have her sent home. I'm going to stay there with her until she passes."

"Shit, Hal! That's taking on a lot. Are you sure about this?"

"Only that this feels like the right thing for me to do."

I withheld the gory details of this undertaking. The more she knew, the more ammo she would have at her disposal to present an argument for why I shouldn't do this. I knew this would only increase my anxiety, but would not change my mind.

Why even go there? Especially, not when my emotions were so raw. And that is where we left things and said our goodbyes.

Puffy cumulus clouds hovered close to the ground. Above them, the sky was brilliantly blue. Sunbeams slipped through the gaps, burning my fair skin as I sat on the Bronco's bumper and made a series of calls.

I scheduled people to come steam clean the furniture. Next, I got in touched with roofing companies and made an appointment with the only one that could begin repairs immediately, that was, if I agreed with their estimate.

Then I did a little shopping, stopping by a home improvement store to buy enough paint for the interior of the house. I decided on wedding cake white. It would certainly take care of the house's dreariness.

Even the cheapest paint, did not come cheap. After purchasing all the supplies that I needed and a trip to the *Food Mart* to stock up on groceries, a serious dent had been made in my wallet.

By the end of the day, I'd applied primer to my mother's bedroom, the hallway, and bathroom. I would get up early the next morning to tackle the rest of the house. Then the walls would be ready for a fresh coat of paint.

That would take another couple of days. I'd really be cutting things close.

Also, I now had an estimate for the roof repair. It was not good news. To replace the rotted areas in the soffit, fascia boards, and the roof deck, and to put on new shingles, it would cost $9,500 dollars.

When I'd heard that they could start as soon as tomorrow, I agreed to it. I arranged to transfer a huge chunk of my savings into my checking account to cover it.

In normal times, I would have sought out multiple estimates. I would have haggled for the best price. But all that mattered to me now, was whether the repair crew had a good reputation and could complete the work quickly.

They did. And they could.

I'd done it now. I'd gone all in, committed myself to a course of action that gave me no choice other than to stay its course.

Still clad in my sweaty paint clothes, I popped a lasagna into the microwave and eyed the rotating glass plate inside. I didn't even own a microwave, but it was here, might as well use it.

I took my dinner to the dining room table and promptly burned the shit out of my chin with a strand of cheese coated with marinara sauce.

While I waited for the pain to reside and for my dinner to lower to a temperature that couldn't melt steel, I went through the drawers in the buffet cabinet.

This was the place where my mother had always stored important documents, birth certificates, you name it; Anything important lived here.

I pulled out a recent financial statement summarizing her retirement benefits. But there were other settlement statements. She'd been receiving $800.00 per month from a trust being handled by the law firm of Chandley & Stewart.

Their logo sat on the top of the page, a solid red diamond outlined by a thin white line, outlined by another red line. They operated out of Nashville.

I had no idea what this could be about. Had my mother sued someone and won some sort of settlement?

My mother was many things, but since we have established that she had never really been a person to take action, more likely to seethe in silence and take it out on the people closest to her, i.e., son or neighbors, that was probably not it.

I made a mental note to call the office tomorrow to get some answers.

The buffet was part of a set. There was also a hutch and a round dining table with 6 chairs. It had been purchased sometime in the 1930's, Jacobean style, oak, made by a local company that no longer existed.

Geometric designs were carved onto the backs of the chairs and onto the other cabinets. I'd always dug their medieval castle vibe. And surprisingly, given the state of the rest of the house, they were all in relatively decent condition.

I found the set of floral, Noritake China that had belonged to my grandmother still tucked away inside the hutch. Other than small chips on a few of the pieces, they were the same as I remembered them.

I wasn't sure why this made me so happy. It wasn't like we had ever used them. Lord, no! We ate from paper plates. Most nights it was boxed macaroni and cheese or processed cold cut meats. Or if my mother was feeling particularly generous, we might actually have a canned vegetable, but that was rare.

Mamma had mostly subsisted on vodka and cigarettes that she partook of as she watched me consume whatever treasure she decided to dish up. One night, she had mixed together a can of chili with the mac and cheese and beamed about it, as if she'd slaved for hours over a Southern Living recipe.

"Isn't it delicious?" she'd asked.

I'd assumed that she'd tasted it at some point to come to this conclusion. It was good. But I was nine. And uh…my culinary bar was set pretty damn low.

I don't think I had actually seen anybody eat a salad until I'd hit the dining hall at UT. Then there was the whole process of teaching myself to like things that didn't originate in a box.

Sandy told me that I had the palette of a toddler and she was right. I kind of did. But within the time I'd been with her, I'd actually grown to like sushi, hummus, salads with spinach and arugula, and to develop a fondness for sriracha chili sauce, that glorious nectar that trickled down from heaven itself. That felt like progress to me.

To be honest, I had always wanted to sit in this dining room with this table set with those beautiful plates and prepared dishes that looked too pretty and perfect to eat. I figured there was a part of myself that must have still clung to this fantasy.

I chanced another bite of lasagna, relieved that it had cooled enough to safely eat without requiring medical attention, and wondered when my mother had painted the room midnight blue.

Maybe it was the same time she'd reupholstered the dining chairs in fabric printed with preening peacocks.

I kind of liked it. This room I would leave as it was.

I hadn't bothered turning on any lights. Earlier in the day I'd stripped all the tattered blinds and curtains from the windows, and now the mood was set by magic hour.

Because I was sitting in mostly shadow, I wasn't worried that the woman, who had stopped on the street in front of the house, would notice that I was watching her.

I thought she was maybe younger than myself. She was slender, of average height, with blonde hair cut into a medium length bob. The woman looked toward the open window as if she somehow sensed that I was here.

She paced in a circle until she arrived back at the exact same spot, threw her arms up, and frowned as she argued with someone.

But who was she talking to, exactly?

Likely, she wore a pair of Bluetooth ear buds and was on her phone. But I had to admit, the way she looked, waving her arms around like that, was a bit insane.

Enough so that it made me chuckle under my breath.

Her voice grew louder, "Joe! JOE! Stop following me! Or I will NEVER help you! You're being a pain in my rear end."

Lady, this Joe person sounds like serious stalker. Get a restraining order and move on.

Abruptly, she broke into a brisk walk and continued on her way down the street. I moved to the window so that I could see where she was going. But a part of me already knew.

She turned onto the sidewalk in front of house #222 and disappeared through the front door.

CHAPTER FIVE

With the sounds of hammering coming from the roof and my paint roller moving rapidly across walls, a somberness fell over the day.

I hadn't allowed myself to explore what was going to happen when all of these preparations were completed. Instead, I fell into the rhythm of them, the completely exhausting pace of them, that made it impossible to think too far beyond the moment.

Then I got the call that brought reality rushing in.

I nearly dropped my phone into a five-gallon bucket of paint before I managed to answer it.

"This is Marc with Tranquility. Am I speaking with Hal?"

"Yes, this is Hal," I said, breathlessly.

"I wanted to let you know that it looks like they will be out this evening to deliver the hospital bed and oxygen. Your mother's medicine is being shipped to her house and should arrive today as well. And do you think you will need a wheelchair?"

This question threw me. Would I? I mean she *was* dying. I hardly thought there would be time left to head out for a movie and popcorn.

"Do *you* think I will need it?"

"Let me see....,"' There was a long pause and I realized I might have just set up a scenario where this poor employee had to weigh the legal implications of a reply to even this simple question.

But I didn't have time for this. I had a house to finish painting.

"You know what, yes! I will need a wheelchair," I said.

"Ok. One wheelchair it is. Tomorrow, your mother's nurse, Nancy Scott, will stop by to get your mother settled in. And Janine Rollins will be by to bathe your mother at some point. She will probably call you to find out which days and what time will work best for you."

"That sounds fine." But there was something in the wording of what he'd said about the nurse that got my attention, "You said, the nurse would stop by to get my mother settled in. Does that mean there will be a different nurse staying at the house?"

"Oh, I'm sorry. Uhm...I guess...I guess Denise did not really explain this to you. Our nurse, your mother's nurse, Nancy, will stop by Monday through Friday to check in on your mother and to make sure she has everything that she needs. But other than that, you will be the sole caregiver for your mother."

I was vaguely aware that I had dropped my paint roller onto the canvas drop cloth. I was sure that I was hyperventilating as I drew in rapid, shallow breaths.

I was pretty damn positive the light headedness I was experiencing was from this and not the paint fumes.

Was this what utter panic felt like?

Shit. Shit, shit, shit, shit.

Things had suddenly become very real.

In the scenario I had pictured in my head, I was a mere fixture in the background. The real, star players were the teams of nurses catering to my mother's every need.

It was the scene I'd seen played out in multiple movies and the occasional soap opera. It was the reason I'd had any expectations at all about how this was going to play out. But Hollywood was a lying bitch.

Marc's voice pulled me from the abyss of panic.

"Mr. Winston? Are you still there?"

"I'm here."

"Are you okay?" he asked.

"No, I'm definitely, not okay. I'm afraid I'm going to need more help than that, Marc." I leaned against the wall and slid down to the floor, not caring that the paint was still wet or that my back was now coated in it.

"Everything is going to be alright. Let me get in touch with our social worker, Rich. He will be able to help you figure some things out. There are private sitters that can be hired to come in and sit. Don't despair."

I heard the click when Marc hung up. Had I said goodbye? I couldn't remember. All that I knew was that I was fucked. Majorly fucked.

I couldn't do this by myself, day in and day out. I hadn't even been able keep a cactus alive. And I didn't have a clue about what taking care of a sick person on my own, entailed.

As far as paying a private sitter, I was sure that would not come cheap. And I was also sure I wouldn't be able to afford it.

I had to call Denise and tell her that this situation was a no go.

I dialed her direct line at the hospital, but it immediately went to voice mail, "You've reached Denise Hoffmann. I am out of the office on vacation and will not be available to take your call. If this is an emergency, pleases hang up and call 911. Have a blessed day!"

A blood boiling anger with Denise took hold. Had she known how naïve I was about this situation?

I took in deep breaths as I waited for this rage to ebb away.

No, she couldn't have. She wasn't evil.

Or was she?

No, it was an error in communication. That was all. It was a simple misunderstanding.

Half-way through dialing the number for the main desk at the hospital, I stopped.

What would I say? I've changed my mind. Go ahead and condemn my mother to live out her final days in some miserable hellscape of confinement and confusion?

How much private care would what I was spending on the roof buy her? Was it too late to stop the workers?

I rushed outside, looking, I was sure, like a deranged mad man, as I took in the newly replaced soffit and the slate grey shingles that gleamed in the sun, covering half of the total surface of the roof.

A worker, closest to me, paused his hammer mid-air and eyed me warily from beneath the brim of a white hat that might have originally belonged to his elderly grandmother.

It wasn't until I let out a long, exasperated sigh and waved defeatedly before heading back inside, that the man relaxed.

We were well past the point of no return.

I crumpled up the piece of paper that I written the number to the hospital on. I couldn't pull the plug. I couldn't fucking do that. I wouldn't do that to anyone. And there was no one else to help me with this.

Suck it up, Hal and finish what you started.

At around 11:00 pm, I did a final inspection of the house before trying to catch some shut eye. The strong smell of bleach had mostly yielded to that of fresh paint. I liked the new wall color. Everything looked fresh and bright.

Most of the living room furniture and nicotine damaged pictures that used to decorate the walls, had been too far gone to avoid being tossed to the curb. Only a steam cleaned sofa and a couple of upholstered chairs remained.

It felt good in this space, a clean slate. All the years of sludge and decay had been cleared away to make room for something new.

But I had no way of knowing what that something would be.

CHAPTER SIX

"The oxygen concentrator is pretty straight forward. Only use distilled water with it and make sure you don't put water above this line here, but also, keep it above the minimum line. This light will come on if there is a problem. In that case, call us immediately. You have this portable tank for back up should you need it."

The technician rolled the reserve tank to the corner of the room, explained how to turn it on, set the oxygen level, and attached a hose, "This is called a cannula, and it's what the patient will breathe through, same as the one that is attached to the concentrator. They will need to be replaced about every 2-4 weeks." He held up a bag that was bulging with extras and placed it next to the tank.

"That's like a year's worth. Isn't that wasteful? I mean, my mother can't possibly use all those in the time she has left."

It was the second time that day that the quantity of supplies had overwhelmed me. The first time was when I had opened the package with my mother's medications and stared back at around eight bottles of pills, each with a two-month supply.

"This is not an exact science. Many patients hang on for a few months or longer. Our job is to make sure that you have everything that you might need," he smiled warmly.

Months? Could that be right?

I had a business to run. I couldn't just abandon everything for that long. Denise knew all of this. She would have given me a heads-up if this were the case.

Relax, Hal. The medical industry is wrought with excess and waste. Don't let it get in your head. It doesn't mean anything, I repeated to myself, over and over until I was convinced that it was true.

My mother was expected to arrive within the hour. There was a knock on the door and a no-nonsense brunette in red glasses and scrubs waited on the porch.

"You must be Nancy," I said.

"Nice to meet you, Hal." She stepped into the living room and dropped the bag she carried onto the floor. "Would you mind if I used your bathroom?"

"Not at all."

When she returned, we engaged in just a few minutes of small talk before she pulled out her tablet and got down to business.

We walked back to my mother's room which now housed a hospital bed and medical supplies. There, she went through all the medications, explaining what they were for and when to administer them.

"If you bury the pills in some applesauce, it will be easier for her to swallow them."

"Applesauce. Got it," I said.

"I will put a catheter in today, so that will make it easier on you. But at some point, we should go over how to change the under-pads on the bed so that you can do that when you need to."

"I spoke with Marc yesterday, and he said there might be sitters who can help out. Do you know how much that could run?"

"There are. I'd say about $20.00 an hour. Rich will be able to give you a list of companies. That's probably the best way to go since the employees have already been vetted."

"Right. Thanks. Wow. That's a lot. But there are individuals who work alone and might be cheaper?"

She put her hands on her hips and shot me her equivalent of stink eye, "There are. But you don't want to draft candidates from the *Quicky Mart* parking lot, either. This ain't something that should be done on the cheap. And your mother comes with a unique set of challenges."

"You've met my mother, then?" I asked.

"Not yet. But I read her chart. She's a combative patient with Alzheimer's disease and a history of violent behavior with medical staff. I'm going to be honest. It will take a special person to agree to sit with her at all."

I wanted to tell the nurse that my mother was hardly in any shape to be a threat to anyone as weak as she was. But she would see for herself soon enough.

My mind was spinning from information overload. Thickening agents to add to liquids to prevent the aspiration of food into my mother's lungs, wound care, oxygen levels, and safety precautions. Open flames were bad. A thing called sundowning was also bad.

Apparently, for Alzheimer's patients, when the sun went down the proverbial party was just getting started. And it wasn't even the fun kind of party. It was balls to the walls with confusion, agitation, and in my mother's case, extremely aggressive behavior that was accompanied by full-blown hallucinations that outdid acid trips during the glory days of Haight-Ashbury.

Nancy's cell phone beeped loudly and she read the text message. "The ambulance is pulling onto your mother's street."

The fullness of anxiety welled up inside my chest. It was the way I'd always been before I had to deal with my mother. I tried to calm the shaky, off-balance feeling, and we spilled out onto the lawn in time to watch the ambulance pull into the driveway.

I could hear the screaming before the paramedics opened up the rear door. This was not the woman I'd been given glimpses of at the hospital. No, this was the person I'd dreaded going to battle with my entire life, the one sharing space in her brain with an invisible demon.

"Help! Help! Give me my phone. I'm going to call the police. I'm being held against my will!"

"Ms. Winston. We *are* helping you. We are bringing you back to your home." The paramedic kept his voice calm and level. He was of stocky with a fantastic, wooly mammoth of a beard.

There was a tall female paramedic on the opposite side of the gurney who wore a deadpan expression and remained unfazed, as if she'd seen it all before. She helped him to slide the gurney out.

Even after glancing around at the tree in the front yard that had been there as long as I remembered, and at neighborhood houses that should have made it clear to my mother that she was in fact home, she continued to shout, "You're lying. You are trying to kidnap me. Help me! HELP!"

I wanted to shout out, *bring me the patient I visited at the hospital, the sweet, pitiful one, the one who looks like a pouty child.*

My mother was red faced, willful. And she was...what had her chart said about her? Combative. Yes, she was that.

The male paramedic tried to ease her worry, "I guess technically, we did originally kidnap you, but now we are bringing you back."

My mother sat upright with absolutely no effort at all, as if drawing strength from her native soil, the same way vampires and paranormal creatures did. And when she looked back at the man, they were the eyes of a woman possessed.

I'd seen this look before and braced myself. There was no way to get to her before what came next. The sound of her palm, making contact with the man's cheek, cracked the air like a thunder cloud.

If there had been any remaining glimmer of doubt that I was getting in way over my head, this had unceremoniously annihilated it.

It took tremendous effort and all of us helping to get my mother inside. I personally had to pry her hands from the door frame, while Nurse Nancy held her legs to keep her from kicking anyone.

By this time, neighbors had collected in the street and were taking in a good show. My mother bit and clawed and screamed bloody murder. I was sure they were all so very, very happy to see her returned home. They'd probably, secretly missed all of this excitement.

I slammed the front door, cutting the entertainment short, and we maneuvered the gurney down the narrow hallway.

As soon as we got her transferred to her new bed, the two paramedics quickly bid us adieu. This left me and Nancy to deal with her on our own.

Nancy shook her head. "Maybe we should wait until tomorrow to try to put this catheter in. She is already so agitated."

"I agree." My mother was a wild thing and no good would come from pushing her even harder. "But what does that mean, exactly?"

Nancy gave me a look. The look said, *OMG, this idiot doesn't know a damn thing and will likely not survive the night.*

And then just as quickly, the look was gone, replaced with slightly, condescending pity, "Remember the under-pads we put down before your mother came? If she wets or poos, you will need to slide whatever is soiled out, clean her off with the wipes, and put down a new one."

My eyes widened in horror as her meaning sank in. I would have to clean up my mother, the way one would clean up a baby.

That meant I would have to *see* my mother. *Naked.*

"OH…NO…I'm not doing that," I said.

Nancy pressed her lips into a thin line and furled her eyebrows. "You don't really have a choice, Mr. Winston. Your mother cannot stay in a wet bed until I come to check on her tomorrow afternoon. In Tennessee, that qualifies as elder abuse. So, suck it up, buttercup."

The room grew quiet as my mother abruptly stopped screaming and zeroed her attention in on me and Nancy. I wondered if she was comprehending the tense vibe between us. I also wondered if Nancy could get away with talking to me that way.

But I knew Nancy was only looking out for the wellbeing of her patient.

"Hal, is that you?"

The two of us turned from our epic, stare down battle, surprised to find a completely different patient there. This woman smiled warmly and reached for my hand.

"It's me, Mamma."

"I am so glad you didn't get stuck in traffic. Holidays can be so hectic. Did the kids come?" she asked.

My mouth hung agape as I struggled to piece together a correct response. She'd called me, Hal, but I didn't have children. Whose children did she think I would have brought? Which holiday did she think it was?

Nancy must have seen that I was struggling because she stepped forward and introduced herself, "Ms. Winston. I am Nancy Scott. I am going to be the nurse taking care of you. How are you feeling? Are you in any pain?"

I was sure Nancy had done this long enough to be able to read the room pretty accurately. And in that moment, she knew that what I needed most, was time to acclimate to the environment I was going to be living in for who knew how long.

My mother beamed at her. "Nice to meet you. No, I feel fine. Would you like a glass of sweet tea. I just made a pitcher."

Nancy went right along with the fantasy, "That's sweet of you, but no, thank you. Maybe next time. Do you think it would be alright for me to put a catheter in. It will make it easier for you since you can't get up to go to the bathroom, and it will make it easier on Hal."

"Of course. I don't want to be any trouble," she said.

I turned away when Nancy lifted my mother's night gown up. The whole situation felt so inappropriate, a situation a son should never have to be in with his own mother. But in just a couple of minutes Nancy was done. And my mother hadn't put up a fight.

"You're a champ, Rita! You're all set," she said and repositioned her in the bed.

Then Nancy spoke to me directly, explaining how to gently guide my mother to roll on the bed so that I could remove and replace the pad that was underneath her when I needed to.

"Eventually, she is going to have a bowel movement. That's an inevitability. Might as well resign yourself to that."

As Nancy made small talk with my mother and began gathering her things to leave, I grappled with the surrealism of the now, all the steps leading me here, and with the nature of Rita's Alzheimer's induced, split personality disorder.

So far, I'd only met two of them, the screaming demon possessed one that I'd known most of my life, and the proper Southern lady who made pitchers of sweet tea and lived to please others.

I actually liked her.

How many more versions of Rita Winston were in there?

"Your mother looks strong. I mean her blood pressure and vitals are almost as good as mine today."

I was surprised by this. Was it normal for a hospice patient to appear so healthy? I watched my mother sip the vanilla Ensure that Nancy had given her through a straw as if she were sitting in a lounge chair on the beach, drinking a Mai Tai.

I forgot myself and almost asked the question out loud. Then I remembered. My mother might understand this and become agitated again, so I let it go.

I asked Nancy a million questions, things she'd already explained and that I already knew, anything I could to keep her with us longer.

But she was no fool.

She was on to me and was not going to let me stall her a minute longer. "I'm off to see my next patient. Call me on my cell if you have an emergency. One that doesn't involve poop, that is."

Even I, as overwhelmed and stressed to the max as I was, could not resist smiling. I wondered if Nancy had a side hustle as a comedian.

CHAPTER SEVEN

The things I knew how to cook were pretty limited. I could rock eggs. Any kind you wanted to throw at me, bring it on.

I was not intimidated by meatloaf. In fact, I'd become sort of a master of it. Regular run of the mill, stuffed, ketchup glazed, fancy glazed, you would swear you had never eaten better.

And of course, baked potatoes. For what would meatloaf be without them?

Like most manly men, burgers and grilled meats of any kind were not a problem. I was also, pretty good at grilled sandwiches.

But that was where the trail went cold and turned into a frightening terrain of things better off never spoken of again.

That's why when my mother turned to me and asked, "Do you think you could you make me that squash casserole like grandmother used to make?"

I answered, without any hesitation, "Sure. I can do that." Because what could possibly go wrong?

First of all, my grandmother died when I was only a baby, so there were no memories for me to draw upon. Secondly, my mother had never in her life cooked a casserole from scratch. I didn't know the word, casserole, even existed in her vocabulary.

I did what anyone would have done. I picked up my smart phone and typed, *squash casserole like grandma used to make,* then I selected the one with the most stars in the reviews.

Afterwards, I threw all caution to the wind, put in a grocery order for delivery, and got down to cooking.

This was not an easy thing to do with someone constantly screaming, HELP ME, PLEASE, SOMEBODY HELP ME, every five minutes.

At which point, I was forced to temporarily abandon the casserole.

There was an adrenaline rush that happened, a spike in cortisol, when someone called to you in that way. You expected to run in to find them at the mercy of a hatchet murderer, or worse.

Instead, what I found when I got there was my mother sitting up like a queen, a demure little smile fixed upon her face.

"What's wrong?" I asked, my heart beating wildly beneath my pecs.

"Oh, there you are, Hal. I just wanted to know where you were."

"Mamma, I've been in the kitchen. Making the casserole you wanted."

"You're making a casserole? That's so nice. Thank you."

After the tenth repeat of this same conversation, I rubbed my hands over my face and took a moment to allow my pulse to settle down before I said, "Mamma, why do you scream like that? Like you are in mortal danger? It makes me afraid that something terrible has happened to you. Could you maybe try to just call out like, *Hal dear, I need you,* in a calmer, less panicked way?"

I'd mimicked the appropriate tone. Then for comparison I called out to her the way she had been calling to me, "HELP…HELP!!! See how that tone, is not necessary since I'm just in the next room and not in another city."

I swear I saw her slightly chuckle at this.

"I guess that was over the top. I'll do better next time," she said.

"Thank you. I'm going back to the kitchen now to finish making your dinner."

To her credit, the next time she called my name, it was actually low and modulated, maybe even pleasant. But gradually we went full circle and I expected I was going to have to get used to having my heart lurch into my throat whenever she called out for me. There was nothing I could do about that.

That was my first lesson in surrendering to the now, a taste of how I was going to have absolutely no control over the pace of things.

There was no part I could replace to make this better. I couldn't put the problem away in a cabinet for three days and forget about it while I figured out what to do, either.

And there was no client to call up to let know that all hope was gone and that they needed to pick up this item that was beyond repair.

We were dealing with a living, thinking person, whose circuit board was suffering catastrophe failure and now had laser beams shooting out of their eyes.

I was now responsible for all the collateral damage that they caused.

It took three hours to finish the casserole. Some of the mishaps were things like sauteing the squash until it was caramelized, and becoming confused and going back and forth between three different recipes.

These things that had almost made me give up and throw everything in the trash, actually made it turn out pretty fantastic.

The last time I'd cooked something for my mother was when I was nine years old. It had been Mother's Day and I'd made pancakes from a recipe I'd found folded up in one of Grandma Ingrate's cookbooks.

They'd been lopsided, oblong instead of round, and charred around the edges, but I'd decided they weren't terrible. With enough Golden Eagle Syrup, I could argue that they were good.

At 1:30 in the afternoon, I just couldn't stand it any longer. I'd already been waiting hours to deliver this cold surprise and I wanted nothing more than to make her happy on this special day.

When I carried the plate of pancakes and a glass of OJ into her bedroom, she hadn't roused. This led me to sit everything down on the night stand so that I could open up the curtains.

I thought this would be a gentle prompting to get her to see what I'd done for her. She'd smile and say something like, *Halby, you did all of this by yourself? You are the best son a mother could have.*

Had I really been that delusional? Had I understood that no amount of kind deeds could morph her into a completely different person? I don't remember if by then, I had figured that out.

She had immediately bolted up, crying out in pain while simultaneously covering her eyes. "Well…hell! What are you doing? I just want to sleep."

She had still worn her jeans and shirt from the day before. The room had stunk of booze.

That's when I realized that I had done something incredibly stupid. All my fumbling around in the dark, had knocked over an open whiskey bottle. It had spilled out onto the floor, but also, onto the pancakes.

"I made you breakfast. Happy Mother's Day," My voice had trembled. I had gazed at the ruined plate in despair, wondering if anything was salvageable.

It hadn't been.

"Look at this mess. Yeah…Happy Mother's Day to me." She had leapt across the bed and grabbed me by the arm, her fingernails drawing blood. "Get this shit cleaned up. And next time you decide to do something nice for me, maybe, don't."

Today, though, she smiled and slowly chewed her first bite of squash casserole. "Well, whatever this is, it's delicious."

Was it like the one my grandmother used to make? Had there ever actually been a casserole or was it something she'd invented? She'd already forgotten the reason I'd made it to begin with.

After only a few bites, she said, "I don't think I can hold any more."

I put the plate down and sat in the chair I'd pulled in from the living room, a plush recliner that had seen better days but was still relatively comfortable. She began to talk about the day she'd had.

There wasn't anything else to do other than listening attentively. Mamma told me that she had worked at the diner all day, that someone had left her a hundred-dollar tip, that she had washed her uniforms. And would I be a dear and hang them out on the clothes line for her?

"Of course. I don't mind doing that. You're tired and need your rest," I said.

"You are a good son. I should tell you that more often," she said, closing her eyes.

I felt a tightness in my throat. My eyes began to sting. I was fucking crying.

I'd waited my whole life for this, but at last, I'd been given a glimpse of the mother I had always wanted her to be.

CHAPTER EIGHT

I'd fallen asleep with my head resting against the steel railing of my mother's bed. I jolted when I felt someone lift up one of my eyelids to peer inside.

My mother leaned over me. Her nightgown was partially off, revealing a long pale scar where her right breast used to be. She'd removed her oxygen, and her remaining foot was draped across the siderail in front of me.

It was one o'clock in the morning.

"Mamma, let's get you straightened out."

I put the oxygen back on her face and stood so that I could pull her arm back through the hole in her gown. But when I attempted to move her leg from the railing, all hell broke loose.

"Just what do you think you are doing?" she asked.

I stated the obvious, "Helping you back into bed."

"Hell…I don't want to get back into bed. I want to get out of bed. We have to go to the store. I need cigarettes." She had the railing in a vice grip and glared at me defiantly. "Aren't you going to help me?"

"You can't have a cigarette, Mamma. You're on oxygen."

"So. What does that have to do with anything?"

"Do you like having eyebrows?" I asked.

"Of course, I do. How stupid!" She rolled her eyes and tried again to get over the rail.

"Then, you won't like it when an explosion burns them off. Oxygen is flammable."

For several seconds, she regarded me with unveiled disgust.

"You're just making that up. Because you want me to suffer, because you don't care about me," she said.

I pointed to the sign that Nancy had propped against the lamp.

NO SMOKING. FLAMMABLE. OXYGEN IN USE.

"Nurse Nancy cares about you. That's why she hung up that sign."

This did absolutely no good. My mother was still hell bent on getting her hands on a cigarette. "Why won't you help me?"

I shook my head, "I can't help you hurt yourself. You are being unreasonable."

"Call Nurse Nancy and ask her if I can have just one cigarette."

"The quantity of cigarettes is not the problem, the oxygen is. Anyway, we are not going to disturb Nancy at this hour. That would be inconsiderate and rude. And we are not going to the store. Nothing is open."

"Don't just stare at me like some dumb, useless hillbilly. Help me up." Her face was red and there was a purple tinge to her lips.

Somehow, she had slyly removed her oxygen again without me noticing.

"Mamma! Again? Please stop taking this off. You need this to breathe properly."

She covered her ears with her hands, preventing me from reattaching the tubing for the cannula. I stood there holding it on her nose for good fifteen minutes, until she simply forgot why her hands were on her ears and dropped them back down to her side.

She leaned back and I retrieved a pillow she had thrown onto the floor and wedged it underneath her head. "Would you like some water?" I asked.

"No, I don't want water. Can I have a milkshake?"

Luckily, I had anticipated this craving and ordered a shit ton of ice cream. This woman loved it more than any human being should. There were times as a child when I wondered if she subsisted solely on vodka and milkshakes.

"I can do that. But you have to promise to be good while I'm gone."

She smiled at me sarcastically, "Well…duh." Like she could be anything else. Like she had not been caught in an aggressive behavior loop for the last half hour.

But I didn't completely buy it. I hovered outside the door and listened for several minutes. She seemed calm, and after a while, I deemed it safe enough to venture to the kitchen.

I scooped ice cream into the blender, added a vitamin supplement, something Nancy had suggested, and the milk. When it was thoroughly blended, I poured it into a thermal coffee mug that also had a lid and a straw, and wrapped it with a paper towel to keep her hands from getting too cold.

But upon my return, I came to a dead stop in the doorway.

My mother sat with both arms held high above her head. In some strange way, she reminded me of the Atlas statue I'd seen once at Rockefeller Center, on a trip to NYC with some college friends.

Only instead of holding up the world, my mother held up two slightly, rounded, baseball sized globs of her feces.

My first thought was, *Oh, HELL, no! This cannot be happening.*

My second thought was, *Nancy is going to have a field day with this.*

My third thought was, *For the love of Pete, how am I going to clean up this environmental catastrophe?*

The moment I had been dreading had arrived. And it was so much worse than I could have ever conceived with my own imagination. I could practically feel my guardian angel behind my back, laughing his ass off.

"Don't move. I am going to get a few things and then we'll get you cleaned up."

"It's not like I'm going anywhere," she said.

Good one. You had to appreciate a good zinger, even during a catastrophe.

I brought in a garbage bag, lots of wet wipes, and donned gloves that Nancy had left for me. Slowly and meticulously, I cleaned her off, all while trying to tamp down my gag reflex.

It took a long time and I was grateful my mother had calmed down and was no longer fighting me. I removed her soiled gown, pads, and sheets, and raised the bed so that I could get her wiped off.

Everything went inside the garbage bag to be thrown away. I was too tired to worry about doing laundry or to care about how wasteful it was.

I took the plastic tub they had left to be used for this very reason, filled it full of warm water, and gave my mother a bath while she lay on her side facing away from me.

She kept her eyes shut and remained very still. I wondered if she had mentally transported herself to another place, one where her adult child had not just cleaned poo off of her bum.

I wondered if this experience was as mortifying for her as it was for me?

Shortly, I knew the answer to this question. A tiny tear rolled from the corner of her eye, then down her cheek.

I began to speak to her then as if this entire incident had never happened, as if we were simply hanging out having a jolly old time, reminiscing over the past. And when I couldn't think of a real memory, I'd made one up.

"Do you remember the time I fell off the roof and you saved me by catching me?"

This was a risk of course. What if she remembered that this had never happened and the ploy only served in propelling her right back into a combative state?

But then she answered without opening her eyes, "Oh, yes. I do. I was so upset with you for making me worry like that. Luckily, I'd been pulling up weeds and was there when you slipped. You were five years old."

"I was six. You were so upset that you spanked me and sent me to my room."

"I felt bad about having to do that. But I wanted you to know how serious it was and for you to never do that again. You were the only thing I cared about in the world, and it had frightened me so. But the angels took care of you. They made sure that I was there."

"I'm sorry for scaring you like that," I said as I slipped a clean nightgown over her head.

"It's alright, Hal. That was the past. How did you get up there anyway?"

"I shimmied up the downspout. I was pretending to be a super hero."

She smiled as I used the control to raise the head of her bed and said, "That was very clever."

I slipped medication designed to help her settle down into a spoon full of applesauce and she took it without complaint. Then I picked up the milkshake and removed the paper tower. It was still cold but not unpleasantly so, "Would you like a vanilla milkshake?"

She beamed with delight as she reached for it, "Thank you!"

I turned off the overhead light, but left the soft glow of the bedside lamp. For background noise, I found an old episode of *I Love Lucy* that she watched as she sipped her drink.

It was after 3 a.m. when she collapsed into an exhausted sleep.

I took advantage of this to take a long hot shower. I'd made a proper mess in the kitchen and was almost tempted to leave it, but decided it would be better to just deal with it and get it out of the way.

This took me a solid hour. I made a mental note to not use so many dishes next time, advice that I was sure I would soon forget. I was almost positive that I had been asleep before I collapsed onto the sofa.

After only one day, I was already spent. That's why I wanted to smash my cell phone against the wall when it began to ring at 8:30am.

"You had better have a good reason for calling me this early."

"Mr. Winston. I'm sorry to disturb you, this is Rich Ellington. I'm the counselor with Tranquility Hospice."

Sitting up and rubbing my eyes, I regretted being so rude. "I'm sorry. It was a rough first night. Call me, Hal."

"I understand. I don't want to keep you too long. I am going to email a list of sitter services to you this morning. I'll also be stopping in to check on you in a few days after your mother has had a chance to get settled in. Please don't hesitate to call me if you need anything."

I hung up and checked in on my mother. She was still sleeping soundly. I made my way back to the sofa and had just closed my eyes when the phone rang yet again.

It was Janine, the woman coming to bathe my mother, wanting to know if her stopping in around 2:00 pm daily would work for me.

"Sure, that should be fine," I'd said, at that same moment a text message came through. Nancy would be here around lunchtime to check on my mother.

It was clear at this point, that I would likely never get a decent night's sleep again, so I gave up and made a pot of coffee instead.

This was a good thing because as soon as it had finished brewing, the Chaplain arrived and graciously accepted the cup I offered.

I moved my blankets and pillow off of the sofa, "Please, have a seat."

He settled in and asked, "Is your mother a religious woman?"

Was she? Did she truly believe in a higher power?

"To be honest. I've never known her to go to church. Growing up, it wasn't something that we did, but last night she spoke of angels. Quite honestly, this surprised me."

"It's not uncommon for people to become more religious as they get closer to death," Pastor Bob said.

"We've been estranged from each other. I cut her off completely when I left home after high school. I never thought I would be in a position of caring for her."

I left out the gory details. I hadn't wanted to smear my mother or influence this man's opinion of her, especially since she was not in any position to defend herself. Let him think I was the ungrateful son. It didn't really matter what he thought of me.

He only nodded. There was no judgement in his eyes.

"Relationships can be tricky. It's up to us to figure out what lessons we need to take away from them. And there is always a lesson in everyone we meet."

I thought about this. What was my lesson in never having anyone remember my birthday? In never hearing a single word of encouragement? Of being struck in the head with a wooden spoon because I'd spilled Kool-Aid on the floor? Or slapped so hard my mouth bled because I'd simply been standing in the wrong place at the wrong time?

What was my lesson in growing up never feeling my mother's love?

But I only said, "I can think of situations where that might not be possible."

"Oh, me too! Horrible things happen in this world every, single day and I wonder, why would God allow this to be? Then I think, I may never understand it because it's not my lesson to learn. Or it is my lesson and I just haven't learned it yet."

"I mean this in the most respectful way, but that sounds like an ambiguous load of crap."

Pastor Bob was well into his sixties. His skin was like smoky quartz, dark and mottled in places, with antique acne scars. But when the sun struck his face, the tones smoothed themselves out, becoming luminous against hair like black ink.

Something caught his eye and he waved at a woman who stood at the screen door. She looked vaguely familiar and then I realized she was the neighbor I'd seen talking to herself in the street.

It was Pastor Bob who got up to let her in, "Molly Owens! What brings you here? Do you know, Ms. Rita?"

"Hi, Pastor. I'm Rita's neighbor. I recognized your car and decided this might be a good time to intrude."

I sat my coffee mug down and stood long enough to shake her hand, "It's nice to meet you, Molly. I heard you were the reason they came to check on my mother."

I motioned toward the empty wing chair. She sat down on the edge of its seat and leaned forward, indicating that she did not intend to stay long.

"Yes. When I didn't see her for a couple of days, I became worried. How is Rita doing?"

"They've released her into home hospice care. Can I get you some coffee?"

"No, but thank you. Hospice care? It's funny. I would have never guessed that from yesterday. Sorry, I saw the whole scene from my window. It took all of you to get her through the door, like she had the strength of Samson." She laughed, then abruptly stopped and cleared her throat.

"Yeah. It was quite the scene." I wondered what type of person Molly was. Was she genuinely concerned? Or was she here to gather information to fuel the neighborhood gossip pipeline?

She seemed to read my mind, staring back at me from the depths of sparkling sapphire blue eyes, and said, "I'm not trying to pry into your business. I really just wanted to let you know that I'm around. I work from home if you should ever need anything."

"Sure. Thanks," I said, maybe a little too curtly.

"Molly is a kind soul, Hal. If she's offering help, it's sincere."

Pastor Bob stepping in on Molly's behalf made me realize just how rude I'd sounded. It had been completely uncalled for. "I'm sorry to be so dismissive, Molly. I do appreciate your offer."

"Really, it's alright. I didn't take offense. This situation has to be very stressful for you. And we are total strangers."

After a few seconds of awkward silence, the Pastor tried to lighten the mood. "Before you came over, Molly, we were talking about the lessons we gain from our experiences. Hal thought my take on things was pure baloney. But I think there is a lesson to be gained from everyone we meet."

Molly considered this, "I have to agree with you, that every person teaches us something about ourselves. I sure hope I don't miss anything. Goodness, I'd hate to get to Heaven and find out that somebody had licked the red right off of my candy and I hadn't even noticed."

Pastor Bob laughed heartily at this, as if it made perfect sense to him. I was glad he understood it, because I sure as heck hadn't.

Was she saying she'd hate to get to Heaven and realize her lessons had gone over her head?

Before I could ask her to clarify, she said her goodbyes. When she shook my hand for the second time, I noticed how soft her skin was. And there was a lingering fragrance after she'd gone, like honeysuckles stuck in the sun on a hot summer day.

Pastor Bob shook me out of my trance. "I should be going too. Would it be alright to stop by again to visit your mother when she's awake? Do you feel this could give her peace of mind?"

"I'm not sure if you stopping by will help, but it won't hurt to try. The worst that can happen is that she shows you the door."

Pastor Bob grinned, exposing ultra white teeth, "It wouldn't be the first time, and likely won't be the last. I would like to add you and your mother to my prayer list, that is, if you don't mind."

"That would be perfectly fine, Pastor."

I couldn't say then that the power of prayer was something I truly believed in. But even so, the idea of it, knowing that someone else in the world was willing to think about our situation, made me feel less alone.

After he'd gone, still waiting for sleeping beauty to arise, I ate a bowl of oatmeal and called the number for Chandley and Stewart.

The receptionist put me on hold and a few minutes later an older gentleman picked up the line. "This is Mark Howard. How can I help you?"

"Thank you for taking my call. My name is Hal Winston and I am the son of a client of yours, Rita Winston. I've come across some statements in my mother's financial records and was hoping you would be able to help me understand the details of a trust. It seems she has been receiving a monthly amount of $800.00 for some time now."

"And is your name on the account?"

"I don't think so."

"I'm sorry, but I can't disclose confidential information over the phone, and certainly, not without knowing whether or not you are authorized to act on behalf of a client."

"I'm in charge of her estate and have a legal right to act on her behalf. I simply want to find out the source of these funds."

"I see. What is her name again?" he asked.

"Rita Winston."

Over the line I could make out tapping on a keyboard. A long silence followed.

"Are you still there?" I asked.

"Yes, I'm still here. Did you say that you are her son?" His words were clipped. Irritated even.

"Yes. You see my mother has dementia and is not able to handle these matters on her own anymore. And I had no previous knowledge of this trust."

"I'm afraid without proper documentation we cannot go any further. Just a moment while I reconnect you with our receptionist." And just like that I was on hold again.

A different woman picked up the line, "Mr. Winston. Do you have an original copy of the Durable Power of Attorney?"

"I have an official copy. Yes."

"Then you can either mail us an original copy or you can bring the copy you have into our office and we would be happy to take a look at it for you and help you with what you need. Is there anything else I can do for you today?" She asked, courteous and to the point.

"No. Thank you."

Not wanting to part with the only copy I had, I called the county and requested two additional copies in case I needed them. One would be mailed to the Nashville office of Chandley & Stewart.

I worked through the list of companies I'd received from Rich. Repeatedly, I was passed along to this person or that person, until I was told that none of their staff were able to handle a patient with my mother's history.

I hung up in despair.

CHAPTER NINE

It was eleven o'clock am when I heard Mamma call from the bedroom, "Halby, where are you? HAL!!! HALBY!!!"

I wondered which version of my mother I would find waiting for me once I got there. I would never get used to the feeling that came from being summoned in such a desperate manner.

And I never failed to be relieved when I got there and found that there was absolutely nothing wrong.

"I'm right here," I said. "Good morning. Let's get your medicine ready and then we can work on getting you something to eat."

"What medicine? Oh, I'm not taking *any* medicine until we talk to the doctor."

I looked up from the medication chart Nancy had created in time to see my mother take off her oxygen and cross her arms across her chest.

I slid the tubing back behind her ears and tried to employ reason, "We don't have to talk to the doctor, Mamma. The doctor already prescribed the medicine for you. You just need to swallow it."

I picked up the spoon of applesauce that held her morning pills and dangled it in the air in front of her face, but she pressed her mouth firmly closed and shook her head, no.

"Why won't you take it?"

She looked at me with incredulous grey eyes. "Because you can't give me medicine."

"Why is that?" I asked.

"Because you're only four."

It was impossible to argue with that. Would I take medicine from a four-year-old? No, I would not. I digress.

I sat the applesauce laden spoon down. "Would you like some coffee? And could I interest you in an omelet?" I asked.

"Yes, that would be wonderful," she said.

I struggled to navigate the rules of engagement dictated by her Alzheimer's disease. It was not okay to let a four-year-old administer medication, but it was perfectly acceptable for them to use a hot stove and possibly set the kitchen ablaze while doing so.

"Is it alright for me to leave you alone long enough to go and make your breakfast?"

"Of course. Why wouldn't it be? I'm a grown woman."

"Right."

She looked calm enough. I lingered, trying to ascertain whether or not she was in the right frame of mind to be left alone.

Ultimately, what choice did I have?

I switched the television channel to world news and set about making a fresh pot of coffee, since I had already drunk the entirety of the previous pot.

I let it sit on the counter long enough to be in the Goldilocks zone, not too hot and not too cold, before taking it to her, hoping the time it took for her to drink it would buy me enough time to prepare breakfast.

She slurped it through the straw and touched her chest with her free hand, "This is delicious. It really is."

I would never tell her that my chef's secret was a vanilla flavored nutritional supplement.

"I'm so glad you like it. I'm be in the kitchen if you need me."

I cracked the eggs into a bowl, whisked them together, and had chopped up mushrooms, tomato, green pepper, and onion, before I was summoned.

"Help! Halby! HELP!!!" She looked relieved when I ran into the room. "Oh, there you are. I just wanted to make sure you hadn't left."

"No. I'm not going to leave you. I'm not going anywhere. I'm making something for you to eat."

"That's right. Sorry."

And this is how it went, a loop that we were stuck inside of that I could not break, no matter what I said or how hard I tried.

It ended when it had run its course. Then we switched to something else, and a new loop began.

She'd taken only a few bites of the Omelet. I'd tried again to get her to take her medicine.

"I think we should wait for the nurse," she had said.

I was relieved when I heard Nancy's car pull into the drive and was already there waiting for her when she got to the door, "She won't take her medicine from me. She says a four-year-old is not qualified to give her medicine, and that she will only take it from you."

Nancy reached into her bag and handed me a sticker in the shape of a police badge. It read, *Official Nurse's Helper, Absolute Authority in the Absence of Nurse Nancy.* "Let's just say we've had this problem before."

"And this actually worked?"

"Meh. It has about a 30% success rate. But if it doesn't work the first time, wait a little while and try again."

I knew her meaning. With dementia, things were constantly shifting. One minute you were standing on solid ground, the next, you were waist deep in quicksand with no clue as to how that had happened.

"Other than that minor hiccup, how did she do last night?" Nancy asked.

"She was up most of the night. I'm not going to lie. I'm already so tired I can't see straight."

"Pace yourself, cowboy. This is a marathon, not a sprint, and you have a long way to go." She looked at my shaky hands. "Maybe lay off the coffee too."

I wanted to ask, in her humble opinion, how long did she think I had to go. But then I realized I wasn't mentally prepared for her answer, so I left it.

"Did she have a bowel movement yet?" Nancy read the expression on my face and almost smiled, but respectfully composed herself before it could fully develop.

Possibly, she was afraid of pushing me too far, lest she break open the dam that would render me into a hysterically useless mess.

"Yes, and I will never talk about it to anyone, not ever. Even if they torture me."

"Congratulations! You got your cherry popped."

Was she even allowed to talk to me this way? I felt like I'd just received a giant wedgie.

Nancy breezed into my mother's bedroom and greeted Rita warmly, "How are you feeling today?"

"I'm alright. I have a little headache," Mamma said.

Nancy finished taking her blood pressure and said sternly, but politely, "That's probably because your oxygen is low and your blood pressure is high. You have to keep your oxygen on and you have to take your medicine to keep your blood pressure down."

My mother looked up at her with innocent, grey eyes, "Yes, I know that."

"When I'm not here, Hal is the absolute authority and you should do as he says. That includes taking your medicine from him when it's time to do so."

"He hasn't even tried to give it to me."

Really, Mamma? Really?

Nancy winked at me and asked, "Would you mind giving your mother her pills now?"

I said nothing and slipped the spoon with her pills into her mouth. Apparently, when Nurse Nancy was around, resistance was futile.

"What have you eaten today?" Nancy asked my mother.

"Oh, I haven't had anything to eat today."

I wanted to contest this, but with dementia, the patient was always right. You were forced to forgive everything, because the moment in question was gone and no longer existed, at least for the patient, it didn't.

Nancy glanced at the omelet that was sitting on the nightstand barely touched, and smiled.

The rest of the day was relatively calm, my mother settled down for a nap, and I used this break to check emails and voicemail at the store.

I wish I could say that I was overwhelmed by all the customers coming my way that were not being helped, but I had no emails and only a few calls. None of the inquiries were even things I could help them with.

I remembered what day it was and that my rent was due. I called the property management office, explained the situation, and apologized. Then I wrote out a check for $1900.00, plus the $35.00 late fee, and carried it out to the mailbox.

It seemed like a good time to catch up on some sleep. I laid down on the couch and slid easily into a deep state of dreaming.

I was somewhere tropical, in a hammock spread out between two palm trees. One of my hands fell over the side and my fingers grazed hot sand. But then something heavy fell on top of me, blocking out the sun. I heard laughter and felt a kiss on my cheek.

A woman smiled down at me with impish delight, but it wasn't Sandy. It wasn't a super model either.

The woman smiling down at me was Molly Owens, smelling of honeysuckle, and the sea, and the sand, and sunshine.

I buried my hands in her hair, lowered her mouth down to mine, but something began to fall over us, and we were both covered in feathers.

All I could hear was the throaty cry of a bird in the distance. It was haunting and steady. And someone was calling out my name.

"Halby! Where are you? I'm scared. HALBY!"

Still in between worlds and unsteady on my feet, I rushed toward my mother's room, "I'm coming!"

"Thank you, Jesus! What the hell took you so long. Your little boy grabbed my car keys off the nightstand and ran outside. You have to stop him."

"Mamma, there is nobody else here."

"He's all alone outside. What if he locks himself in the car? It's so hot, Halby! Please, go and get him."

"Mamma, I don't have a son. We're alone here."

"How could you be so stupid to forget that you brought him. It's irresponsible. Lord, please, let him be alright! You have to go find him!" She wrung her hands in desperation.

Her oxygen was off which might have been feeding these hallucinations.

I reached to put it back on, but she swatted my hand away and glared angrily, "What is wrong with you? He could be in the street by now."

"I'm going, Mamma. But you have to put your oxygen on first." I slid the cannula back on her face. "Wait here, I'll be right back."

"Hurry! Hurry, dammit!" she screamed and I could see that her hands shook nervously.

At the end of the hallway, I leaned over, bracing my hands on my knees. *WTF?*

I knew it would be better to just play along. But how did I do this without making things worse?

I went out into the front yard, standing near the window where my mother was, and shouted at no one. "Little Hal, you come here, right now. You are upsetting your grandmother."

Then I went back inside, letting the screen door slam loudly behind me, and shouted to the invisible boy that was causing so much trouble, "Stay here! You're in time out, mister. No, you're not having ice cream with grandma later. I don't care. You heard what I said."

Back in my mother's room, she drilled me, "Did you check him over?"

"I did. Not a scratch. He's fine."

"You didn't have to yell at him," said the woman who once threw a hot skillet at me.

"Why are you upset with *me*? If he thinks it's all just fun and games, what's to stop him from doing it again? He's in time out, and lucky, I might add, that I didn't spank him."

"Well, maybe later he could have some ice cream with me. I'm sure by then he'll have learned his lesson," she said. "And anyway, it's not like he fell off the roof."

Another zinger, a pretty good one at that.

"Hey. That was a low blow. Don't you go giving that little hellion any ideas. It's time for your medicine."

This time she took her pills without complaint and leaned back to watch an afternoon talk show.

The aide arrived late, "I'm so sorry. I know I said I would be here at earlier, but I got held up with a patient."

It was no problem at all because I had forgotten all about her coming today.

Janine was a softspoken person with a gentle and soothing manner. She maneuvered effortlessly around my mother, washing her body and hair with a warm pan of soapy water.

She changed the sheets and switched her dirty gown for a clean one. I marveled at just how easy she made it look, and how quickly she was done.

After she'd left, I turned to my mother, "Are you hungry? There is leftover squash casserole and we have frozen lasagna in the freezer."

She wrinkled up her nose. "That doesn't sound good to me. I would just like a milkshake. But only if little Hal can have one too."

"Alright, if you promise to drink every drop."

"Yes, I can do that."

As far as I was concerned, little Hal had it too easy. But who was I to interfere with the bond between a grandson and his grandmother.

CHAPTER TEN

We had both fallen asleep with the television on. I awoke in the chair and could feel the change in air molecules, as if something vast, hungry, and dark had sucked energy from the room.

My mother had both knees draped over the side of the bed. Her left big toe almost brushed the floor. The shrinker sock that should have covered the area that had been amputated, had been pulled off.

I realized that it was my fault. I had forgotten to put the railing back up earlier when I'd adjusted her pillows.

But it was the way that she looked at me, the sarcastic smirk lifting up the corners of her mouth, that alerted me that I was staring back at the same woman I'd left behind on the eve of my high school graduation.

Everything about her demeanor instantly repelled me. I had to still the urge to flee, to get as far away from her as quickly as I possibly could.

Her voice was gravelly and abrasive, a scouring pad that scrubbed at something stubbornly clinging to a cast iron pan, "Stop being lazy. Get over here and help me!"

Instantly, I slid back in time, back to when I was very small and helpless, to a time when I had no choice but to face the woman that I was terrified of disappointing in some way.

The only difference now was that I was a grown ass man. And this woman, even this version of her, could no longer be held accountable for her actions.

"Let's get the railing up so that you don't fall." I made a move to slide her legs back onto the bed and felt the sting of her fingernails digging into my forearm.

I looked directly into her eyes, mere inches from my own, "Stop, clawing at me. It is not okay to hurt people just because you feel like it."

"What did you tell people about me all these years? That I'm a monster? And what have you done with my letter?"

"The one that I wrote, telling you to fuck off, the one you kept framed on your nightstand, that letter?"

"Yes. It's my property. Where is it?"

The day I'd found it, I'd dropped it inside her top dresser drawer. But I was in no mood to feed into this argument, "I'm sure it's around here somewhere."

"Give me the phone. I'm going to call the police. I am going to tell them that you've stolen all of my things and trapped me here," she rocked back and forth in a frenzied agitation.

"Alright, let's call them, Mamma. You can tell them all about how I paid to put a new roof on your house out of my own pocket. How I came in and scrubbed shit off of your walls, and painted the whole house. If you are lucky, they might even take you back to the psyche unit that I rescued you from."

She pursed her lips as if weighing whether or not there was any truth to what I was saying. And then she simply changed the subject, "I want to walk to the living room."

"You can't walk on your own anymore."

"Then help me, dammit!"

"No, not while you are acting this way and attacking me. It's late. We should both be sleeping. If you agree to get back into bed and to take your medicine, then I'll agree to make a plan for getting you out of bed for a bit."

"It's not right, holding me in a cage like this," she said, but then she threw up her arms in a sign of surrender and allowed me to reposition her in the bed.

This time I made sure to raise the railings and lifted the foot of the bed to a slightly higher angle, one that would make it a little more difficult for her to escape.

She fumed silently, watching while I dropped a pill, intended to help calm her when she became distressed, into a spoon full of applesauce. "How do I know it's okay to take this?"

"Because there is a chart that tells me what I can give you and how often."

"Let me see the damn chart," she said.

"By all means." I handed it over to her, waiting patiently for her to read or pretend to read, each item.

She handed it back, "Shit! I guess I'll take them now."

She opened her mouth for the spoon and I watched to make sure that she actually swallowed them and wasn't just squirreling them away in her cheeks.

Then I wrote down the time I'd given them to her.

"Is that a cigarette in your hand?" she asked.

"It's an ink pen."

"Oh. Do you have any cigarettes?"

"I don't smoke, so no."

She mimicked my reply and rolled her eyes. "There's some money in my purse. Take your bike, and get me some cigarettes. Go on now!"

It took a few seconds to process the way the details of her mind had merged, past and future intermingling on the same plane.

"It's three am. No, I won't do that. And also, you can't smoke….," I pointed to the posted sign, remembering that this particular personality had not been made aware of it yet. "Because, you know…you might blow us both to smithereens."

"Don't sass me! I'll smack your damn mouth in. You'll do as I say."

I ignored her, sat back down in the chair, and turned the channel to a sitcom rerun that I was unfamiliar with, dropping the volume until it was only white noise.

"Pfft…useless, as usual," she seethed.

"Mamma, why did you frame that letter and keep it all these years?" I asked.

She didn't look at me. "As a reminder, that the only person I can count on, is myself."

"Doesn't it get lonely, Rita Winston, always fighting against the world?"

"You think you had it so bad." Her fingers went to the faded, starburst scar. "When I was three, my daddy came

97

home drunk and decided to put his cigarette out on me while I slept. A broken collar bone when I was four because he knocked me down, a little too hard. I watched him hurt my mother, leaving bruises all over her. All I could do was cry and suck it up because nobody stepped in to help us, even people who knew what was happening."

Looking at the scar, it was suddenly, so obvious what had caused it, that I was shocked and confused that I had never really put this together.

It made me question my own perceptions about my mother, the lens that I viewed her through that had filtered this out.

She'd never spoken directly about abuse she'd received as a child. Although there had been hints that my grandfather had not been a good person.

I knew that her father's name had been Norman, and that my grandmother, Ingrate, had met him at the front door with a shotgun one fine, summer day after receiving a visit from a woman claiming to be his wife.

The woman had driven all the way from Pasadena, California with divorce papers. Since the house had been in Ingrate's name and their marriage hadn't been legal, she had decided she didn't owe him one minute more of her life and had kindly offered not to blow his brains out or to have him arrested for polygamy if he never darkened her doorstep again.

But I should have seen the deep pain that my mother carried inside. It had such a dense presence that it orbited her, the atoms of this pain organizing themselves into a hard exterior shell.

"I'm sorry that happened to you. I wish you would have talked to me about this."

"Why, so that you could point out that I turned out just like my loser of a father?"

"No. Talking about and acknowledging the things that have hurt us, is the first step in healing those things. Maybe you wouldn't have spent so many years on this planet angry about what you couldn't control if you had."

She looked at me smugly, as if to say, she still knew all the right buttons to push and had no qualms about pushing any of them, "Is that what you learned in college? I guess, you hate me just like I hated my father. And I suppose I'm responsible for ruining your life and everything bad that ever happened to you."

"I don't hate you, Mamma. I just decided I wasn't going to spend any more time living inside of your toxic bubble. But the only person capable of ruining my life, is me."

Saying those words out loud felt strange. I felt the power of them soak into me, like I'd released a subconscious thought into the wild that I hadn't even known was there.

But were these words true?

My mother seemed to sense this momentary doubt, taking it for weakness, and decided to test me by pushing even harder, "I never wanted you. I swore I would never bring a child into this terrible nightmare of a world. But then I messed up and got pregnant. I was stuck."

"Did you think that not wanting me was some kind of secret? You don't think that never giving me a minute of your time or giving a shit about anything that happened to me, gave that away?"

My mother began to laugh. It was cynical, broken up by fits of coughing, the product of too many years smoking and lungs damaged by COPD.

I couldn't help but note that even her voice was different when her body embodied all the memories of her life.

It was when she forgot her past, when she was released from the judgement of others and herself, that she became a thing of light and was able to embrace a joyful state of being.

"Mamma, why do you think your neighbor is a witch?"

"Oh, her! Because she's always talking to spirits in front of my house. It creeps me out."

"I think she wears Bluetooth earbuds when she talks on the phone with someone you can't see."

"I can see them."

"You can see these spirits?"

"Duh…that's what I just said."

I'd attended a lecture while at the University of Tennessee, called, *Honoring Faith and Protecting the Dignity of the Dying Patient*. It was given by a retired doctor whom had spent 35 years working as a surgeon.

I couldn't remember the name of the book or the doctor's name, but one of the chapters that he had discussed, had drawn a lot of excited questions from the crowd. It had concerned experiences when patients were near death and was possibly the only reason that I still remembered it at all.

The doctor had shared what he had found to be common, patients seeing loved ones that had already passed over to the other side and having hallucinations, even when they had never had them before.

One of the questions from the crowd had been, "Do you think they are really seeing spirits?"

Laughter had erupted, but the doctor had been unfazed by it, "I have given much thought to this. Of course, the answer to this question is, that I simply don't know. My logical mind tells me that these things are impossible, but the spiritual part of me and the emotional part of me, believes that these patients are seeing what they say they are."

A girl in the back, who had worn lots of bracelets and bright orange lipstick, had stood and urged him to elaborate more, "So you think the state of being near death, allows us to see into another dimension, like Heaven?"

"As a man of faith, I don't think this is a strange concept at all, that our savior would try to make this transition as comforting as possible by sending familiar faces to greet us. Next question please, one that doesn't involve spirits," he had said, regaining control of his lecture.

I thought about the little boy that my mother had seen that I could not see. As far as I knew, before the dementia my mother had never had hallucinations either.

But would God have sent a little boy that had never existed to comfort her? Who had he been? And what had put the thought into my mother's mind that he was my child?

As for the spirits surrounding Molly Owens, I was curious if my mother recognized any of them and asked.

"Only one, he sort of looks like…,"

"Sort of looks like? Tell me."

"Your father," she said.

Of all the people she could have dredged up, that was the last person I had expected. Mainly, because I had never been able to get her to talk about him before.

She hadn't bothered to include his name on my birth certificate. Trust me when I say that it is not a great feeling to have, name unknown, instead of a father listed on a document you have to present throughout your entire life.

I had pressed her in the past, always with the same results. "He was a sorry, good for nothing grifter, just like your grandfather was. And you are better off not knowing anything about him," she would always say.

"Do you think my father is dead?" I asked, hoping I would get a different response now.

"I know he's dead," she said.

"How do you know this?" I asked.

My mother was already closing her eyes and seemed to have forgotten what we were talking about, "How do I know what?"

It was 4:30 in the morning. I should have just let this all go and gone straight to sleep myself. But I hadn't been able to.

For my whole life I'd had a theory about my conception, that my mother was actually a succubus in human form. That she had snuck into some unwilling man's bedchamber and taken advantage of him, an unforeseen consequence being that she had also received his seed.

Behind this logic was a disbelief that anyone would willingly choose to be intimate with her. Not because she was unattractive, she wasn't, she was beautiful and tall, with a natural elegance in her movements that didn't quite match her disposition or circumstances.

I thought this because she was hard, judgmental, and cruel. And I couldn't imagine anyone being drawn to her to begin with. Which was probably why I'd never pushed for more information about the man I shared DNA with.

I mean, if my mother thought he was bad news, what sort of person were we dealing with?

That was a whole bag of icky I hadn't wanted to go poking around at.

Let's just say for argument's sake, that the spirit of my father was actually hanging around the neighborhood waiting for my mother to die.

If he had been a horrible person and bad people went to Hell, did that mean he was waiting around to escort her there?

It didn't feel good to think that my mother might be doomed to a place of never-ending torment, fire, and brimstone.

I mean, she had devoted her life to being as toxic as Chernobyl, but I didn't hate her. In spite of everything, I knew that I loved her.

The other question was, why would my father's spirit be following Molly Owens around? How could she see him?

Did I even risk asking her about this?

Those were the kind of questions that could get you locked up for good.

Even if I had wanted to know more about my father, there was nobody around to press for it. My mother had no friends. We had no family left. It was futile and would only lead to dead ends.

What I really needed to do was to shut my brain down long enough to get more than three hours sleep, and when I couldn't do that, I picked up my phone.

I'd turned off the volume and hadn't heard several text messages come in from Sandy.

I just had a steak dinner out and it felt weird to be eating your favorite thing, without you.

If you get a chance, please call me and let me know how you are doing. I've missed you.

I'm going to sleep now. I'd hoped to hear from you. Or at least for you to let me know that you are still alive. Jesus, Hal. Please just let me know something. Anything.

I didn't want to hurt Sandy. But I didn't want to talk to her either. Making time for pleasant chit chat when I was this tired, was something I was not motivated to do.

There was guilt connected to this. This was the woman I loved that we were talking about. Truth be told, my instinct hadn't been to lean into her for support. Honestly, I didn't know how to do that.

Sorry, Sandy. I really am. I am fine. There isn't time enough time left in the day after caring for my mother. It takes a lot out of me. Oh yeah…and did I mention that hospice only comes by for a short time each day to check on my mother and I can't get any sitters to stay with her because they say she is combative and they are not equipped to deal with that kind of patient. I shouldn't complain. I took this on of my own free will. I sure miss sleep, though. And most of all, I miss you. I will call you when I get a chance.

I hit send, then dragged an ottoman from the living room, took my pillow from the couch, and curled up in the chair in my mother's room. Spending time with my mother when she was like she was tonight, made everything so much more difficult.

All of it was mentally exhausting, the figuring out how to navigate the constantly shifting sands of the subtle and outright changes in her moods and personality.

But the angry person who resented everything and everyone, she took the prize for most joyless and soul sucking.

I wasn't sure which personality would return when my mother woke up, but I sure hoped it was the sweet little lady who liked my "special" coffee, and seemed to have genuine gratitude for these simple gestures.

I understood that little lady was actually a facet of my mother. Did she represent the best parts of her that had been suppressed for so long, suffering in solitary confinement all these years?

And had it only taken the devastating impact of disease to set her free?

CHAPTER ELEVEN

Two weeks in, my mother's health took a sudden and dramatic dip and she had been sleeping almost two days straight. She had hardly drunk or eaten anything. Enough so that Nurse Nancy showed me how to administer morphine should the need arise.

It was a Thursday when she pulled me out of the room and told me that she believed this could be it. "If she does not improve by tomorrow, I'll come in over the weekend to check in on her."

I was bit devastated by this. My mother looked so frail. I used one of the green sponges that Tranquility Hospice had provided to moisten her mouth.

Janine had skipped her bath on Wednesday, but this morning, bathed her without Rita even stirring.

A few hours after Nancy had gone, my mother opened her eyes for a brief interval. She smiled at me and reached for my hand, "Thank you for being here. You are a good son. And a good father. I was not a good mother to you, and I am sorry for that."

I felt tears well up in my eyes. My throat constricted as I squeezed her hand back. I didn't bother correcting her and pointing out that I was not a father and likely never would be.

She had apologized.

She felt remorse.

She remembered hurting me, without becoming an evil sadist to do so.

"It's alright. You did the best you could, Mamma." I realized that I meant it.

Rita Winston had not been able to climb out of the pain caused by the things that had happened to her and that pain had had controlled her for most of her life.

But here in this moment, she was not that woman. She was Rita, sent from an alternate dimension to right the wrongs of the past.

"From now on, we'll make some better memories," she said.

"Of course, we will," I said through tears. And then she was gone again, back into the deepest sleep, to a place where no one could reach her.

Later that same evening, I noticed that the temperature in the house was rapidly rising. The air conditioner had stopped working.

I located some fans to place by Mamma's bed and opened up every window in the house. Then I pulled a small tool box out of my Bronco and went to the backyard to look at the unit.

The weeds had long ago claimed it, wrapping around and enshrining it like some ancient relic. I spent the better part of twenty minutes clearing them away and swearing under my breath, only to discover just how much of an ancient relic it was.

I guesstimated after noticing all the built-up gunk on it, that it was at least 20 years old. That was shocking to me since I figured it might have been that long since the thing was actually serviced. Like myself, it seemed to have been running merely on a wing and a prayer.

After removing the fuse, I unscrewed the panel that housed all of the wiring. I stared down at the twisting interconnected network of red, brown, black, purple, and grey wires and sifted through the files of useless information stored in my brain.

What did I remember about air conditioning systems, evaporator coils, liquid refrigerant, and blower fans?

In the midst of this system check, I realized how sleep deprived I was. Constantly stopping what I was doing to check in on my mother, was not helping matters.

For the first time in my life, I didn't even try to fix the problem. I gave up and searched my phone for an air conditioning repair company.

As luck would have it, the guy only lived a mile down the road. When I explained the situation with my mother, he said, "I'm just finishing up my dinner. I'll be there right away."

But the news Dale delivered upon arrival, was not good.

"Honestly, I think this unit is done for"

"And how much to install a new one?"

He scratched his head while he did some calculations.

"I'd say about $3500.00. And I could have it installed first thing in the morning."

Great. That was just what I needed, another huge expense eating away at savings I couldn't afford to lose.

"Do you accept checks?"

And just like that, poof, it was gone! If this trend continued, I would be bankrupt in the very near future.

I washed up, figuring that I should try to eat something, although I didn't have much of an appetite. I definitely, should have tried to catch up on my sleep.

But I couldn't. Every creak and noise coming in through the opened windows drew me back to check on my mother.

I contemplated making a pot of coffee as I ran my hand over my chin. I didn't mind the new growth of a beard. It actually felt appropriate. I was a man trying to survive the wilderness of mental illness while keeping my own sanity intact, a man kept going, solely by the miracle of caffeine.

The quiet rap on the screen door surprised me. It was almost 8:45 pm, only just beginning to grow dark.

Molly smiled at me from the other side, holding a Pyrex dish in her hands.

"Please, come in," I said.

"I had a whole basket of peaches I needed to use, so I made you both a peach cobbler."

I took it from her and couldn't stop staring into her sapphire eyes. For a few seconds, I was lost there, but then I remembered myself, "Thank you. How kind. I was about to make coffee. Would you like to join me for dessert?"

"That would be great." She followed me into the kitchen.

The room swelled with her presence, making me hyper aware of her. When I reached around to get to the drawer of flatware next to where she stood, I was immediately struck by the floral scent of her shampoo.

It was amazingly pleasant. So much so that I had to fight the urge to pick up a strand of her hair to bury my nose in.

"How is Ms. Rita today?"

"She's declined over the past couple of days. Her nurse is concerned."

"I'm sorry, Hal. And how have you been holding up? This can't be easy for you?"

"It's not. As you can probably tell from the new, stranded in the wilderness, look. I've completely let myself go."

She smiled, "I kind of like the rugged look."

She moved closer to the window and leaned into the breeze. It blew her hair back, reminding me of a model in the midst of a fashion shoot.

Molly was not beautiful, and yet, she was. It wasn't in a typical way. There was a girl next door vibe, a natural wholesomeness, but there was also a splash of the mysterious about her. Something exotic that was not easily explained.

"It's a little hot in here," she said.

"Sorry. The air conditioner quit today. I would offer you a fan but they are all in my mother's room. Speaking of whom, I should probably, check on her. I'll be right back."

"Take your time."

Checking on Mamma was really an excuse to get out of the kitchen long enough to gather my wits about me. I wasn't sure if it was the dream that I'd had about Molly Owens causing these runaway thoughts, or if I really was attracted to her.

I mean, she was attractive. But I was in love with someone else. The odds of these feelings going anywhere were pretty much zero.

My mother was just as I'd left her. The only difference being that she had closed her mouth and curved into more of a fetal position.

When I returned, I found Molly in the dining room spooning cobbler onto plates she'd taken from the cabinet behind her. I followed her lead, taking out the delicate cups and saucers that matched, and brought in the pot of coffee.

It was high time somebody used this room.

I wondered where this sudden jolt of energy had come from. It was so easy talking with Molly this way, and it had been painstakingly difficult talking to Sandy earlier this morning.

"I want to apologize for all the trouble my mother has caused you. And I'm very happy she didn't flatten you with the lawn mower."

112

"You heard about that. I guess you know better than anybody that your mother's mind is like an attic full of angry racoons."

I had been taking a sip of coffee when she said this and it sprayed out through my nose.

Molly quickly added, "I didn't mean to offend you. Sometimes I open my mouth and things fly out before I realize how they might come across to others. I only meant that she is troubled. She lashes out because she doesn't know how to do anything else. Like a computer program that's stuck in a loop."

I wiped my nose with my napkin and said, "No offense taken. I don't think I've ever heard a more accurate assessment of her. I appreciate your honestly, Molly."

"The offer still stands. I mean, if you need someone to help you. I wouldn't mind sitting with Rita to give you a break for a few hours here and there."

"You would do that?" I couldn't help drawing a comparison to my last conversation with Sandy.

Sandy was concerned, yes, even angry about the situation and lack of help for me. She was going to look into whether not offering services to my mother because of the nature of her illness was discriminatory in any way.

But she had not offered to come to me, to physically be present for me.

"I would be happy to do that for you and your mother."

"Normally, this would be the part where I warned you about what you would be getting into, but you already know that. Thank you."

Who was this woman willing to help out a perfect stranger? What went into shaping such an altruistic soul?

Molly's attention went toward the doorway and she smiled suddenly, as if acknowledging someone's presence there, "I didn't know you had a child here with you. Is he yours?"

I'm sure that my face went as white as a winter's snow. Chill bumps ran the length of my arms.

"You saw a child? It's just that my mother saw a child recently, a little boy, but he was only a hallucination. She thought he was my son. I'm not even married, and I definitely, do not have a child. But how could you see him too?"

With this question, her face became guarded. It was as if she had been caught in something and had to figure out a diplomatic way to explain something that was not so easily explained.

Molly sighed and said, "I was hoping for you to get to know me a little better before I revealed this to you. But I'm just going to say it and hope you don't find it disturbing, some people do. I'm a medium."

Now, in all honesty, if someone had told me a month ago that they were a medium, I would have smiled politely and said something like, "Oh, really. Isn't that interesting," but secretly I would have thought that person was either a charlatan out for money or delusional and in need of medication.

Tonight, I was intrigued, "Can you describe the child you saw?"

She nodded, "Blonde hair. Around four or five years old. He looks a lot like you. I think it's the shape of his lips, and his nose that makes me think that."

Which could explain why if my mother saw this same child, she could have mistaken him for my son. *And what the holy, mother Mary, Hal. There was no child. This was pure lunacy.*

Still, I was curious to find out what Molly would say and asked, "Is he still here?"

She stood, her chair lightly scaping across the floor, and closed her eyes for a moment. Opening them again, she headed out into the hallway, as though she'd caught the trail of something.

At my mother's room, Molly stopped abruptly and gasped in surprise.

That same moment my mother propped open groggy eyes and patted the bed with her right hand, "Yes, little Halby, I'll be up soon and we can spend some time together."

Mamma's hand settled down and I rushed in to rest my own hand on top of it, "Mamma, who are you talking to?"

"Your boy," she said. Her eyes drooped shut again and she no longer responded.

I let out the shaky breath I'd been holding and turned toward Molly, "Would you like to explain to me what just happened?"

"The boy wanted me to follow him so that he could show me something. He jumped into Rita's bed. But when he laid down next to her and slid his hand under hers, she could sense him there."

"But whose child was this and why is he here?"

"He was very happy that I could see him. And he said that he enjoyed visiting his granny."

I rubbed my eyes, wondering if lack of sleep might have left me susceptible mass hallucination and deception. But looking into Molly's eyes, overflowing with concern for me, took all of these thoughts away.

She had nothing to gain from deceiving me. She was truly concerned about how this was impacting me. For now, I had to concede that there was something going on beyond what I was able to perceive.

"I'm an only child. I don't have any siblings with children. I'm on good terms and still keep in touch with everyone I have ever slept with, so no surprises there."

Molly bit her lower lip, before she quietly, said, "I don't think he's been born yet."

I grabbed Molly's arm and pulled her deeper into the hallway just in case my mother could hear us. "What the fuck, Molly? Explain."

"I think he's in limbo. Like he's waiting around to be born. Very impatiently, I might add."

"If I'm the father of this future child, let's ask him who his mother is."

Molly gulped and lowered her eyes to the floor, "I can't. He's already gone."

"Then let's call him back."

I was beginning to think this mischievous spirit child was trying to get back at me for putting him in time out.

"It doesn't work like that. Spirits show up when they feel like it. I don't control them."

I stared back at her, not bothering to hide my annoyance, "So a spirit child operates pretty much like a regular child."

She chuckled. "Yes. That is probably safe to say."

We were very close to each other in dark hallway. I was not even conscious that my fingers were wrapped around her elbow until she shrugged away awkwardly and said, "I should be going. Thank you for the coffee. And don't worry. It will all make sense to you some day."

I walked her to the end of the driveway and watched until she'd made it safely inside her house. The funny thing was that even with the strangeness of the evening and knowing what I now knew about her, it did not change how natural being with her felt.

And those funny little random things she said, I would call those kernels of zany wisdom, *Mollyisms*.

Back inside, I cleaned up the dishes and put them away. For the first time in days, I sorted through the stack of mail piled on top of the buffet cabinet.

Some of it was my personal mail that had been forwarded here. Most was junk mail, but the last item was a large manilla envelope from the county Clerk and Master's office.

I took out a copy of the documents I'd requested and set it to the side to be mailed to Chandley & Stewart.

The trust was a puzzle I hoped to have an answer for soon. Why was there a trust? Who set it up? And where was this money going, because it wasn't showing up on my mother's bank statements. She barely had enough money coming in to cover her medical expenses.

It was time to find a semi-comfortable place to take a nap before this small window of opportunity closed to me.

CHAPTER TWELVE

In the early morning hours, my mother woke with a start and the coughing fit began. It was accompanied by a wet, gurgling sound coming from her chest

There was an anxiousness, a panicky wildness in her eyes that came from not being able to breathe properly.

I raised the head of her bed to an upright position and texted Nancy. She instantly replied that she would be here as soon as she could.

Not long after, I was relieved to hear a knock at the door, but it was only the repairman, letting me know that he was going to begin installing the new unit.

By the time Nancy did arrive, the episode had passed and Mamma was sitting up comfortably, as regal as a queen on her throne, ordering me around.

Nancy made a sour face when she listened to her chest, "I think you may have a touch of pneumonia. We'll order an antibiotic which should help with the infection. Otherwise, your vitals are better than mine are today. You have rebounded with a vengeance, Ms. Rita."

When it was time for Nancy to leave, I walked out with her, "Is this a normal thing, for people to jump back from such dire straits? I mean, maybe she isn't really going to die."

Nancy looked at me squarely. "You must have mistaken me for an all-knowing deity?"

Yet again, I wondered if she could get away with speaking to me so bluntly. But then, I realized she had summed up the situation perfectly.

Neither of us knew what the future had in store for us, any more than we knew what it had in store for Rita Winston.

"It's unfair to expect you to have all the answers," I said.

"Listen if I could tell you how this was going to play out, I would. I could give you a million scenarios that would break your heart and a million more that you would never believe in a million years. But there isn't a day that goes by that something doesn't happen that I have not expected to."

Her tone softened and she placed her hand on my arm, "So do yourself a favor, will you, and try to live in the now, and only in the now."

"Did anyone ever tell you that you are a pistol?" I asked.

"I'm not everybody's flavor, I'll admit that. But honesty is the only weapon I wield. And you will always get that from me." Nancy blew on her gun finger, then slipped it into an imaginary holster as she walked out the door.

I wondered if she knew how much some people feared the truth and what a powerful weapon it actually was.

Mamma's appetite returned with a vengeance. She dictated a shopping list for Spiegel's, mentally walking me through this familiar grocery store. It had closed twenty years ago, but I didn't bother to point this out.

"When you go through the door, the bakery will be on your right. I would like a couple of donuts, one vanilla crème filled and one chocolate."

The list also included T-bone steaks, red snapper, and random things, like 100-watt lightbulbs, paper clips, a bottle of wine, and rat poison.

I was confused about why she needed the last item. "What is the poison for?"

"For the rats upstairs. I heard them walking around up there last night."

There was no upstairs and I had heard no such sounds.

"Anything else?" I asked.

"Get whatever you would like for yourself, of course. And please, don't forget the pecan praline ice cream."

Ice cream was clearly a staple of life for Mamma and on some days, the only thing she would eat. There was no way I would forget that.

I heard the air conditioning kick on and was relieved to feel cold air flowing from the vent next to my chair.

I took a moment to close all of the windows, and settle up with Dale. Then I used my phone to place the order for delivery, ordering everything she wanted except for the poison.

We spent a large portion of the day, chatting away, the way old friends did whenever they got together to reminisce. I was a person that she had lived another life with, one that only she remembered.

When she asked me questions, I invented details that logically went along with her narrative.

"Do you remember when we used to take the boat out at night for picnics?"

"It was always my favorite time to spend with you. I loved looking up at the stars, and you would point out all the constellations, like the Big Dipper and Pegasus," I said.

"The water was so still and quiet. We would huddle up in our blankets and eat fried chicken, corn on the cob, and fried cherry pies. That one time we drank a whole jug full of sweet tea that kept us up all night long."

Then she began to laugh, holding her stomach as if it were painful for her to do so, "And that one time when you nearly caught the boat on fire."

I laughed too. This was a challenging curve ball, a dramatic and unexpected twist. "You'll never let me live that down. It was ambitious to think that two people could send up a hundred Chinese lanterns at the same time. But you acted quickly and smothered it out with your blanket."

"It still has a hole in it," she smiled.

"You have to admit it was something, watching all those lights floating in the sky above us, the way they reflected on the surface of the lake."

"It was magic," she said.

The sentiment took me aback. How had this woman, the same person who had always been filled with so much anger, anger that fueled a never-ending furnace of violent rage, draw this word from the cosmos?

But that is what this moment was. It was pure magic that had been carved out of a fairytale.

I took advantage of Mamma's nap to finish putting away the groceries that had been delivered.

When the baking potatoes were nearly done, I fired up the coals and cleaned off the grate on the grill. Tonight, we were having a feast, steak, red snapper, and a salad. It was entirely too much food for us.

And thanks to Molly Owens, there was also cobbler for dessert.

With thought of Molly came the urge to run over to her house right then and invite her to eat with us. But that was a very bad idea.

Mainly, because of the way my pulse accelerated whenever she crossed my mind. And I wasn't sure how my mother would react to the person she perceived to be the neighborhood witch suddenly showing up in her bedroom.

Mamma's face brightened when she glimpsed her dinner, "Is that for me?"

"It certainly is." I slid a tiny piece of the T-bone into her mouth, followed by a small bite of baked potato that had been loaded with butter, sour cream, and sprinkled with chives.

She chewed slowly, savoring every morsel with a look of pure satisfaction.

It had taken half an hour but she ate everything on her plate. When I offered cobbler, she accepted excitedly, closing her eyes after tasting it, "Now, this is truly delicious."

"We have Molly Owens to thank for dessert."

"Do I know her?"

"Molly is your neighbor, Mamma. She lives in the little green house down the street, the one with the beautiful red roses out front."

"*Oh*, the witch. That was nice of her."

"Yes, Molly is a very nice person."

"Well, she would have to be to make something as sweet as this."

"Exactly, so maybe cut her some slack in the future. It hurts her feelings when you call her that."

"That's what little Hal said too. And then he explained everything to me."

I wondered when this conversation with little Hal and my mother could have occurred since he had fled the scene when I'd demanded more clarification on his origin story.

And now not only did my mother and Molly see this child. They had me playing in to it too. "What exactly did he explain to you?"

Mamma shook her finger at me, the way one did when they caught someone trying to pull the wool over their eyes. "Ah-ah-ah. That's a secret."

If this little Hal kid ever came into existence, I was going to ground him for life. "It's certainly not okay to hide things from me."

My mother looked at me sympathetically, as if all the wisdom of a sage was bound up inside of her, "I can't tell you, Halby. Because it's not your time to know."

After long minutes of rephrasing the question, going in at different angles, and still not drawing this mysterious secret out of her, I let it go and went to the kitchen to clean up the colossal mess I'd made.

I reflected on this day of ease, of things effortlessly falling into place, a day that made going with the flow feel like second nature.

The thing about these moments though, was that while inside of them, there was a pervasive feeling of permanence to them, like things would always be the exact way they were right then.

If suffering through some horror, it felt as if it would never end. And on those days filled with joy, it felt so light, like it too would last forever. And the possibility of anything changing, didn't seem inevitable at all.

CHAPTER THIRTEEN

Sundowning was a plight visited upon mankind by the most evilly minded demons, from the deepest and most fiery pits of Hell.

It was like traveling through a category 5 shit storm without so much as a raincoat for protection.

It was the farthest thing from a miracle that one could ever imagine, a secret government experiment carried out upon the population to test the limits of sleep deprivation.

And I was pretty sure that the pills in the bottle of medication designed to combat it, were actually sugar pills and nothing more.

In other words, they were useless. Completely and utterly, useless.

There didn't seem to be any predictable timeframe or pattern to it, other than that sometime between the hours of when you needed to sleep and when the sun rose, the person suffering from this affliction would awake.

And when this happened, we were not talking about a little restlessness, a little tossing or turning, or watching television into the wee hours. Nope, this was something else.

The term *sundowning* sounded so poetic, like a stroll through the park to catch the sunset, whilst holding hands with a lover.

I decided a better name, pulled directly from the movie, *Highlander*, was, *the quickening*. Only there wasn't any beheading involved, just the extraction of energy, the caregiver's energy.

It gave the patient supernatural powers of endurance and strength. It was the time when my mother turned into a person I actually, sort of recognized.

It was when she remembered all the shitty details of her life, the ones that had shaped her into an angry and bitter person. It was when she delivered insults and the occasional right hook, or worse.

That brought us to the poop incident.

But, Hal, we already know about the poop incident. It was in a previous chapter…

No, this was something different. Let me set the scene.

My muscles burned and ached from pure over exertion. There was a splitting pain in my temples from only sleeping six out of the past 48 hours.

Somehow, I'd managed to nestle myself inside of a cozy dream. It felt so nice, that I decided that I was simply going to stay there, hiding out from all the things I didn't want to face. Perhaps, I'd never have to wake up again.

Then the universe caught wind that I was feeling a bit sorry for myself, that I was being a whiney little bitch, and decided to show me that I had a thing or two to learn about my own levels of endurance.

I heard a distressed scream. Was it part of my dream? No, my dream was pleasant. This was something else.

When I was able to pry my eyes open, I discovered that Mamma had gained enough willpower to somehow haul herself over the rails of the rented hospital bed. She was sprawled across the floor, a projectile of urine and shit, spraying out in all directions.

Alert now, I realized that 1) she had pulled out her catheter and that 2) she had diarrhea.

But this was not the average run of the mill diarrhea. No, it was something else, a dark, sticky, tarlike substance that that clung to her skin and refused to be washed away.

I sprang into action, approaching the situation the way I might have approached an item someone had dropped off for repair. I stripped it away, layer by layer, assessing, prioritizing, and fixing it.

Then, when that was done, to the very best of my ability, I put everything back together into a kind of order.

There was a big difference between a thing and a person. A thing didn't cry or scream out in helpless desperation. They didn't tell you that you were the worst thing that ever happened to them. They didn't claw at you until you bled, or fight tooth and nail as you attempted wade through the foul mess at hand to rectify what was wrong.

In the aftermath of these incidents, there was always a sigh of relief, that I had made it through them. Whatever they were, whatever distressing situation had happened, they were over.

And in a strange way, this made me stronger and more prepared to face the next one.

I made a promise to myself that I would not allow myself to develop PTSD from any part of these circumstances I found myself in, that I would find at least one thing to be grateful for in them, one thing that would carry me through. I would ride them like waves, surrendering to what was.

On this particular night, I was grateful that my mother had not been injured, that I had been able to clean her up without breaking open sores on her delicate skin. I was grateful that she did not seem to be in any pain.

Also, having a sense of humor hadn't hurt either.

I was grateful that my mother's aim was not so great and that the poop she had begun to hurl toward the ceiling, had not reached its target.

CHAPTER FOURTEEN

From the distance between us, Sandy fumed, "You can't keep up this pace. You need a break. You need to come home, Hal!"

I wasn't sure which thing Sandy was more upset about, my wellbeing or not having me around for companionship.

But there had been a hopeful development. Nurse Nancy had recently told me about a thing called, respite care.

It was a Medicare benefit designed to give caregivers a break. For five days they would take my mother to a facility and I could go my merry way during that time, doing whatever, whenever I pleased.

Complete freedom. Ahh.... that word had a wondrous ring to it, *freedom*.

The problem was that after a little time spent looking over my mother's medical history and seeing the word, combative, again and again, we were having trouble finding a facility that would agree to take her, even for that brief time.

"That has to be discrimination, a violation of the Americans with Disabilities Act. I'll call the representative for Piney Valley. We'll get the politicians involved. Let them know who they are fucking with. We'll sue them if we have to."

I had almost forgotten what a bull dog Sandy could be. I mean, it wasn't a side to her that I got to see very often. It was mostly reserved for her battles in court, going after good for nothing parents who refused to follow the terms of custody agreements, or to pay child support.

Outside of court, it was reserved for people who didn't follow proper societal etiquette. This usually happened when she was driving, like someone taking a parking spot that she had obviously been waiting on, or cruising in the left lane of the highway as if it were that person's private lane and not a legally designated passing lane.

On our second date, Sandy had insisted on driving. She was a skillful driver. Really, she was. But she liked to drive fast. I mostly, remembered gritting my teeth as she revved up the engine of her Volvo and aggressively passed slower drivers on the highway.

And when a clueless driver blocked the left lane, preventing her from passing for ten minutes, she found a way to get beside them, only to shame them by honking at them, calling them idiots, and shooting them the bird.

She was absolutely, terrifyingly, ferocious when she needed to be.

"I don't have the strength or money to take that on. I'm going to have faith that something will become available in due time. What I could really use now are your prayers that a solution will present itself," I said.

Not that I hadn't had my own pity party. As of late, I'd had some pretty dark days, days where I looked at my situation and wondered why my life was going up in smoke. But mostly, I wondered how I would recover financially.

I became angry at the world and wanted to punch holes in things. I wanted to break things and rage against the dark cloud that was following me.

But that never truly made me feel better.

What did make me feel better was when I found within this heap of stinking negativity, some tiny thing that I could be hopeful about.

"I can't promise that I won't look into things on your behalf." Then she added, "I want to see you. I would come there but I don't know if that's a good idea considering my feelings about your mother. I can't trust myself not to suffocate her with a pillow for all of the evil things she did to you in the past."

I laughed at her attempt to lighten things up. It was funny in a dark, Sandy way. It was also sad. And I wasn't sure which was more so.

I tried to picture Sandy in my mother's house, looking at old pictures, eating with me in the dining room, the way I had with Molly, or sitting with me at Mamma's bedside.

I couldn't see her there at all.

It was strange to realize that the person I'd spent years with was not actually a person I felt comfortable with when things slid down hill. And I wasn't sure what that meant.

Was it just this situation and all of my childhood wounds that made this so? Or was it something else?

Then I thought about little Hal. Could this child become a reality from a union between us? Would Sandy somehow soften, decide she actually did want the house, kids, and the complete package society always wanted to push people toward?

Would I ever be enough for a person like her?

But instead of delving into those things with her, I said, "Thank you, Sandy, for everything you're doing behind the scenes. It means a lot. I'll call you again, first chance that I get. I promise."

"You take care of yourself."

"I will."

I wondered if she had noticed that I hadn't told her that I loved her. In fact, I hadn't the entire time I'd been gone. But then, neither had she.

It was something that we had always done when we kissed and said our goodbyes in person.

In the past, when we talked on the phone or even texted each other, it was usually things like, *feeling like Thai food for dinner, what do you think?* Or, *could you pick up some eggs on your way?*

We just didn't do the flirty, affectionate banter that other couples did. I had always put it down to our having atypical love languages.

Lately, though, when we spoke, the conversation was strained. She struggled to understand my situation and to find ways to support me from a distance. Her efforts felt a little like misplaced guilt.

But I also carried guilt, for dreading these conversations with her. There just wasn't a lot left of me at the end of the day. I was tired of pretending with her that I had it all together.

I sensed that any hint of wavering moral or the fact that I was barely getting by day by day, would drive her crazy. And so, I protected her from it all by avoiding having these conversations altogether.

It had been many days since I mailed the documents to the law firm in Nashville. I checked in on my mother and after realizing she was still napping, decided to give them a call.

"Hello, this is Hal Winston. I recently mailed something to your office and need to get information on the trust that was set up for my mother."

"Hold on for one second," a young woman with a kind and professional Southern accent replied. When she returned, she said, "I found the document you sent, Mr. Winston. What information did you need, exactly?"

"Well, I don't know what this trust is. I mean who set it up for my mother?"

"I'm sorry to have to place you on hold. Please, give me a few minutes to track down these records."

I drummed my fingers on the dining room table and stared out of the window as I waited. I noticed the first signs of yellow leaves with their curled-up edges, falling like origami from the trees.

It was September, and I realized that fall was almost upon us. This thought filled me with sudden anxiety.

I did not have income coming in and yet I still had the same bills to pay. My savings were barely on life support. My days were spent inside the bubble of my mother's house while time slipped away from me.

Mamma was still going strong. In fact, she seemed every day to be getting stronger. What that meant for the future, I was not sure. But I'd committed to this, to seeing that she was taken care of. For the time being, I didn't see that I had any other choice.

When the woman returned, she said, "I'm sorry you had to wait for so long. It was set up back in 1986 by one of the partners here, a Mr. William Chandley, but there is nothing that specifies why he set the trust up to begin with."

That was the year I was born. Could this person have set this up for Ingrate before she died, distributing what was left of family wealth? But why not just turn it over in one lump sum? Why set up a trust?

"Forgive my confusion, but who was it that Mr. Chandley set this up for?"

"Let me start again. Mr. Chandley set it up using his own money. I don't think anybody here now would know anything about it. Mr. Chandley was in his sixties when he did this, and all the original partners, who would have known about it, are now deceased."

This did not make sense. My mother did not have any family left, especially not rich relatives in Nashville who would have left her money.

Who had this William Chandley been to my mother?

"This is still confusing me. Would you mind digging into this a little more? Maybe, you could talk to the remaining partners. I would be extremely grateful for your time."

"Alright, Mr. Winston. I will see what I can dig up," she said reluctantly.

"There is one other thing, I see that my mother receives statements for this but it's not being deposited into her bank account. So where is this money going?"

"It goes into a savings account. But I'm not allowed to give you this information over the phone."

"I understand." I read the numbers to Mamma's account out loud, "Does that match what you have?"

"No, that does not match our records. I can't say anything else over the phone. You will have to make an appointment to come in and meet with one of our attorneys. We will be more than happy to help you clear this up."

"I understand. Thank you for your help. What was your name?"

"I'm Tracy. And you are very welcome. I'll be in touch if I have any new information for you."

This was truly a mystery. Who knew when I would be able to get away to travel all the way to Nashville. I hadn't had a single break in over two months.

If I were being entirely honest, I was beginning to fray a bit. The non-stop pace, of never getting a true moment to myself, or knowing when I would get to rest, was becoming more and more difficult with each day.

I needed something to break up the monotony of my days. I needed human interaction beyond this place. Even when I talked to Sandy, I felt alone in what I was going through.

"HELP! HELP!"

As usual when my mother called out for me, there was the rush of adrenaline, a major spike in my cortisol level.

My logical mind told me that when I reached her, she would be perfectly fine, like she always was. It told me that I would find no real danger when I got there. But knowing this, did not stop my body from reacting, every, single time.

I knew some of this spike had a great deal to do with an overbearing dread about which personality I would encounter.

Would I find mean Rita? Warm and compassionate Rita? Or a morphed-up version of both?

Would we be in the present, the past, or would it be some fantasy version conceived from the depths of my mother's imagination?

To be honest, I kind of liked this last version. I never knew what adventures we would be going on.

Would we be sneaking out of a fancy Paris restaurant because she forgot her wallet and was afraid that they would send us both to jail for speaking with Southern accents?

According to Mamma, Parisians hated all Southerners with a purple passion. Where this idea came from, I haven't a clue. I just went with it.

Would we be invited to sing onstage with Elvis at Madison Square Garden again?

Would we be taking the sailboat out today? Piney Valley was now prime ocean front property thanks to global warming.

It was escapism in its finest form. Some days it was something to look forward to. Some days it was the only thing keeping me from tossing the toaster into a bathtub full of water and calling it a day.

I'm not going to lie. There were times when I felt so depleted that this seemed like the only way that I might get some relief.

That's how dark things got for me. But then that elusive thing deep down, that tiny spark of hope, kick started my battery. And I was back, as good as new, connected to the land of the living.

When I reached Mamma, she was sitting up in her bed, all bright eyed and bushy tailed, smiling up at me as if she had not just been screaming bloody murder, "There you are. I was afraid you had left me alone."

"I haven't gone anywhere in months. I am always here, watching over you, every day and every night, like a stalker."

"I forgot," she said sheepishly.

How had I even been annoyed by this? She had Alzheimer's.

I felt terrible whenever I lost patience with her. When she struggled to grasp something or in those moments when she recognized that she was not remembering things that she should have known, I also felt terrible.

"No worries. I made a fabulous lasagna. Would you like some?"

This was a warping of truth. I hadn't made anything. I'd warmed it up from the stock pile of frozen dinners that I kept in the freezer. Today, I simply didn't have the will to cook.

"I don't think so. I'm not very hungry."

"Milkshake, then?"

Her milkshakes always included vitamin supplements so I was always happy when she would at least drink one of these.

"That might be OK," she said. Her attention went to the foot of her bed and right away she became distressed, "Please get these bugs off of my blanket. Hurry! Before they bite me."

I quickly rolled up the pale blue, crocheted blanket and rushed it from the room. In the hallway, I made stomping sounds loud enough for her to hear and tossed the blanket into the laundry before grabbing a clean one from the linen closet.

I found it was just easier to go along with these hallucinations and to manufacture the quickest remedy possible for relieving her anxiety.

When I draped the clean blanket over her, she began to sob with a soulful sadness.

"What's wrong, Mamma? I got rid of all the bugs."

"I don't want to be in this bed anymore. I don't want to be in this place. Please stop torturing me and let me go home."

"You are home. Look, that is your dresser, your lamp, your chair. These are all of your things."

"But this is not my bed. It's a cage."

It was a keen observation. It essentially, was a cage, configured for her maximum comfort, but also to make sure she wouldn't be able to climb out of it again and hurt herself.

"Mamma, we are renting the bed. It's better for you right now. And I'm sorry that you feel like you are in a cage, but we have to keep the bars up so that you can't fall out."

"I would just like to walk to the kitchen, dammit. Is that so hard for you to understand? Just help me!" She glared at me angrily, already swinging a leg over the railing.

"Ok. I have an idea. You tell me if you think it's a good idea. If you drink all of your milkshake, I will take you outside when it gets dark and we will look at the stars."

She stopped struggling and studied me intently, "You're just saying that to get me to eat something."

"No, I'm giving my word. I promise. If you keep up your end of the deal, I'll keep up mine."

She nonchalantly, slid her leg back off of the railing and settled down, "Can we do the lanterns again?"

I smiled, amazed that she had remembered this conversation and been able to pull it from some mixed-up filing cabinet in her brain.

"I don't have any lanterns today, but if this goes well, we can try to do that next time."

What in the world was I committing to? Where did one even find Chinese lanterns? How did one do such a thing without sending the entire neighborhood down in a blaze of fiery glory?

Before I could take it back, she said, "Ok. Deal." And extended her hand for me to shake.

Now to make a milkshake and to figure out how in the hell I was going to get my mother outside by myself. This was probably a very bad, no good, idea. With any luck, she would forget all about it soon.

But the instant she had finished slurping down her milkshake, she looked up at me expectantly.

"Not yet. We have to wait until the sun goes down."

"Right. Right. We can't see the stars when the sun is out. I forgot."

I left her with the nature channel on, steering clear of news that would definitely be full of depressing things, and figured out a plan of action.

Portable oxygen tank. Check. Wheel chair. Check. Clear path to navigate through. Check. Something to prop the broken screen door open with. A strap to secure her into the chair so that she would not fall out.

I used the weed eater to clear a spot on the lawn. The monkey grass was knee high, even higher in places where

141

the dandelions had crept in. I was sure we would receive a citation from the city any day now.

I knew I should just buck it up and take care of it, on one of those days when she seemed to sleep endlessly. But doing something as simple as mowing the grass, felt almost as difficult as climbing to the peak of the most difficult mountain.

I couldn't bear to think about it, let alone, commit to doing it.

As soon as the stars appeared in the night sky, I looked over at my mother, "Are you ready to go outside?"

"Oh yes, I am. Are we going to church now?"

Church? That was such an odd thing to associate with my mother. We never went to church. We never talked about religion.

Growing up, the only times I had seen the inside of any religious institutions were when I had a slept over at a friend's house on a Saturday night and got dragged there on Sunday morning by default.

But I knew that Ingrate had been deeply spiritual, a life-long Southern Baptist, so I could only assume this had been a regular ritual to her childhood.

"No, not church. We're going to look at the stars," I said.

"Alright. Now? I don't have on my coat." She stared down at her arms, bare in her short sleeved-nightgown.

"That's alright. We'll take a blanket for you to wrap up in. I'm going to lift you now, and then I'll swing you into the chair."

142

She only nodded, letting me know that she understood.

With my arms wrapped around her securely, I lifted her as gently as I could, pivoting so that she could be deposited into the wheelchair.

She appeared relaxed as I secured the foot pedals and tied the strap to ensure there was no way that she could slide out. Lastly, I attached the portable oxygen tank to the chair.

I had given up on the idea of getting her out of the back door. There were fewer stairs but that stoop wasn't structurally sound. I hadn't wanted to risk it.

That left the front yard and being in plain view of prying eyes. But I didn't care. Let them think whatever they wanted to.

Just wait until the day that we unleashed the lanterns. Then they really would have something to talk about.

Getting her out of the front door wasn't without its challenges either. I didn't trust the railing and therefore, could not lean on it for support. And it was narrow.

I tilted her chair back and took things slowly. Each time the wheels bumped against another step or there was the slightest wobble in our trajectory, my mother would cry out in terror and I'd have to take a few moments to reassure her that she was safe.

We made it. I was out of breath and my mother clutched her chest as if she had been through the most traumatic ordeal imaginable. Other than that, we were both unscathed.

I pushed her to the five by four-foot square of grass that I'd cleared for us and wrapped her with the blanket, even though it was 80 degrees outside.

With a silent reverence, we took in the intense black of the sky, breathing in the scent of newly cut grass.

"Where is the moon?" she asked.

"There's a new moon tonight."

"Then it's a good night for stargazing," she said.

I looked over, expecting her to be staring up at the tiny pinpoints of starlight that loomed overhead. Instead, she watched me with an earnest expression on her face, "Do you hear that sound?" she asked.

I heard the steady trilling of summer insects, the clumsy, bellowing, mating calls of frogs, and the intermittent rush of cars on a nearby street.

I wasn't sure which sound she was referring to, "You mean the crickets?"

"No, not that," she held up her finger, a cue for me to wait for something that was to come. When a mournful call rose into the night, she said, "That."

"What is it?"

"A whippoorwill. That sound, *whip-poor-will*, is where the name comes from."

I listened carefully and again the same haunting sound penetrated the air. It sounded as if it were perched in the tree at the edge of the yard.

"I don't think I've ever noticed it before."

Presently, it was my predominant focus.

"When I was little, my mother told me that when you heard one sing out close to the house, it meant someone was going to die soon."

In the darkness, I could barely make out the deep lines of concentration that spanned her face. I thought maybe there was something more to it, a recognition of what the sound could mean for her. Perhaps she understood that she was on a collision course toward a fate that this omen was predicting.

We hadn't talked about the fact that she was, according to her diagnosis, in the last stage of her life. I wasn't sure if anyone, nurse or doctor, had ever delivered this news to her directly.

I certainly hadn't wanted to have this conversation and avoided mentioning words like, hospice or dying, in front of her.

But even when she had given me the perfect opening to find out, I just couldn't go there, "That just sounds like silly old folklore."

She shrugged, as if it were of little consequence one way or the other, and glanced up at Orion's Belt. She lifted her hand and made a motion as if invisibly drawing a line with her forefinger to connect the three brightest stars.

For a second, I thought she had forgotten, but then she said, "I'm afraid, Halby. I'm afraid of what is going to happen to me."

The rawness of her vulnerability, paired with astute momentary clarity, caused a lump to begin at the back of my throat and a stinging sensation in my nose and eyes.

145

A tear broke free, making a freefall to my jaw. I turned away, discreetly wiping off the wetness, and pretended to pluck a weed from the ground before I answered, "Don't be afraid, Mamma. There is nothing to be afraid of because I'm here to watch over you."

"Thank you, Halby." Her smile was filled with such saccharine sweetness that I could hardly bear it.

I feared I would be reduced to a sobbing fool. I held my breath, focused on the haze of light pollution in the sky, and slowly exhaled. Then it felt safe enough to offer her a reassuring smile.

I gently squeezed her hand, and we sat there for a long time, wading through our own silent thoughts, enjoying the cool breeze that steadily blew in.

I thought this was the best window of opportunity, I'd had so far, to bring up the topic of Chandley & Stewart. "Mamma, do you know anything about the trust that was set up for you?"

She fixed her gaze on a large oak tree in a neighboring yard and answered without looking at me, "Yes, of course I do."

"Why did a Mr. William Chandley decide to give you money?"

At the mention of his name, a shadow fell over her mood and she looked troubled. But she didn't answer.

It dawned on me that there might be a correlation between this trust and my birth, "Mamma, was this man my father?"

She began to laugh then, but it was more of an expression of disgust, "Absolutely not. How could you even think I would have anything to do with that evil old man? That wily snake in the grass. He took everything from me. Nothing that he could ever do would make that right."

She rubbed her arms in irritation and squirmed in her wheelchair. With an abrupt sour tone, she said, "The mosquitos are eating me up. I'm ready to go home."

Unwittingly, I'd hit a nerve. I had sent her spiraling into the past, back into what Molly had referred to as, the attic full of angry raccoons.

But if this man hadn't been my father, then what had he done all those years ago to cause her so much pain? And how did I get answers without forcing her back into all of that pain?

"Alright, Mamma. Let's get you inside."

I turned her chair around and prepared for the treacherous trek back up the steps. I glanced toward Molly's house.

Warm light beckoned to me from every window, but I knew it had more to do with the warmth inside of Molly Owens. It was the way she held space for love and kindness, and it was so freaking bright that you could feel it radiating from a distance. It was a beacon in my small little world.

For a second, I thought I saw one of the curtains move and a silhouette slip behind it. Had Molly been there, observing us just now?

I looked forward to the next time we crossed paths. And maybe, just maybe, she could help me gain answers about what had happened to my mother in the past.

If this William Chandley was in the spirit world, and Molly Ovens was a bona fide, true to life, medium, then she might be able to reach out to him for answers.

I wondered what the going rate was for a channeled message from the other side. Hopefully, it would not break the bank. But whatever the cost, I was willing to pay it. I just hoped she felt comfortable enough to do this for me.

By the time I got my mother back into her bed, she was breathing heavily and looked weak. She had seemed so strong as of late, I was surprised how this mini trip had taken so much out of her.

But it had all been worth it, just to give her this small piece of happiness, regardless of how short lived it had been before it had been stolen away by the past.

I rubbed some antihistamine cream on her arms but could find no evidence of mosquito bites. She was already falling into a deep sleep, leaning on her left side as she always did.

CHAPTER FIFTEEN

Pastor Bob picked a day to stop by when my mother was awake. She was the model hostess, joking with him and telling him a story about the time she snuck a guinea fowl into church with her and it laid an egg right on top of the pew.

"Before I could catch it, it rolled out into the aisle," she said.

Now whether this had actually happened or not, who could say? But it had the pastor roaring with laughter.

With each sidesplitting outburst, her story grew more and more outrageous, "Before I could get to it, Rodney Peterson, took it and slipped it onto Brother Pinion's chair. I never liked that boy. He was a freckle-faced trouble maker."

"Well...what happened next?" he asked.

"That was part one. We'll save part two for next time," she said, leaving us with a cliff hanger.

"Ms. Rita, you are an interesting character. I have so enjoyed visiting with you today. I hope you don't mind that I added you to my prayer list."

She reached out and squeezed his hand, "I appreciate you doing that."

With his free hand, Pastor Bob gently patted the hand that held his own and leaned closer to Mamma's ear, "Just remember, God has you in his arms. He'll take care good care of you."

"And Halby takes good care of me too," she said.

"That he does," he agreed and winked at me.

I followed him outside, but he stopped on the porch and turned to take a good long look at me, "Son, please don't take this the wrong way, but you aren't looking so good these days."

There was no offense taken. I had eyes. And there was a mirror in the bathroom that reflected back the dark circles, gaunt cheekbones, and the woolly beard that was starting to go the way of a ZZ Top impersonator.

There was also a scale in there and I knew I had lost ten pounds that I didn't really need to lose. "It's the newest trend. It's called, survival chic. All you have to do to get it, is to take a trip with your dying mother through the American medical system. Only the lucky survive. They should offer me a reality television show," I said.

"I'd laugh if it weren't true, and so sad. We've got to get you some help up in here."

"Save it. She's a handful. To be honest, I can't afford to pay for sitters."

"I spoke with Rich Ellington about you. He's trying really hard to find a place for your mother so that you can get a break for a few days. Some place is going to come through for you. Try to keep the faith," he said. "But in the meantime, you have someone right down the street, put smack dab in the middle of your path, yet you ignore that help."

"You're talking about Molly?"

"Who else? The Lord does watch over idiots and fools." He waved his finger at me and climbed into his late nineties model Buick sedan.

I wondered if he thought I was the idiot or the fool in this scenario, or both. But he was right. I did need Molly's help, but for my own reasons.

By late afternoon, Mamma's mood had turned dark. She gripped the bedrails in a way that would have made a free climber envious, and tossed her oxygen cannula angrily to the floor.

Then she began to hurl insults at Janine, "Get your hands off of me, you stupid cow. Help! SOMEONE! She's hurting me."

Janine paused from removing Mamma's gown for her bath and looked to me with slight frustration. From behind my mother's back, I mouthed, *I'm so sorry.*

To my mother, I said, "It's not okay to call people names. Janine is a sweetheart. She would never do anything to hurt you. If you don't want a bath, that's fine. I'm sure there are people out there who actually need her help and won't abuse her." I picked the cannula up and repositioned the tubing behind her ears before tightening the chin strap.

"Good riddance, then. Let her go and ruin somebody else's day."

Janine had to quickly cover her mouth to hide the smile that broke out. When she regained her composure, she said, "Ms. Rita. I'm going to go now. We'll try to have your spa day another time, alright? You have a wonderful rest of your day."

"Spa day, my ass," Mamma said before flipping her off.

Janine only raised her eyebrows and bit down on her lower lip. I was glad she could see the humor in the situation, my mother with her gown halfway off, leg hiked over the railing.

Her hair was a tangled-up mass of silver that stood up like a crown of thorns around her head and she had refused to let either of us brush it. The entire time Janine was there, my mother pouted like an insolent toddler and acted out like an absolute bohemian.

For the rest of the day and for the next twelve, solid, non-stop hours, things went just like this, like a pile of steaming shit wrapped up inside of an enigma, inside of another giant pile of shit.

Until 3:00 am rolled around and Mamma at long last, decided she would take her pills. Then she passed out, I was sure, from utter fatigue.

There was a quiet buzzing in my ears and I wondered if it was the sound of my brain cells slowly dying. Unless, of course, it was an aneurysm. In that case, I was done for.

My last thought before sleep was, would that be a fortunate outcome or a negative one? It was an argument that I could have easily argued both sides of.

Also, did that make me a realist, an optimist, a fatalist, or a pessimist?

CHAPTER SIXTEEN

Mother had just gone down for a nap. She was already snoring, a deep nasal snarl that made me think of rabid dogs. I figured I had at least 10 minutes to make it to Molly Owen's house and back again without being missed.

Her garage door was open and I could see that her cream colored Mini-Cooper was parked there. Good. She was home.

I rapped lightly on the front door with my knuckles. Too lightly. I tried again. This time pounding my fist. I decided that I'd done this too aggressively. The knock sounded desperate. Probably, everyone on the block had heard it.

A few seconds later, the door swung wide and Molly stared back at me, smiling like a ray of sunshine from the best kind of summer day, the kind that included shaved ice, sand castles on the beach, and catching a double feature of your two most favorite movies of all time, right after finding out you had just won the lottery.

It was that kind of smile.

"Hal! Hi, come in. Is everything alright?"

Temporarily, I forgot why I'd knocked on her door to begin with, then said, "Uhm...I was hoping that if you had time later, you might like to come over for a beer. I need your input on something."

She eyed me warily before inviting me in. "Is this about the little boy I saw?"

Her front door opened into a sitting room—polished hardwood, a large area rug with geometric patterns of vibrant orange, red, cream, and navy blue, and turquoise walls.

There was a long narrow table against the wall. It was covered with an Indian sari and filled with unusual things. I drew closer to it.

"No...not about that," I said, but I was distracted by what was on the table, noticing an array of feathers.

One of them, from a peacock, the rest, three in total, from a red-tailed hawk. There were crystals of various compositions. Some I recognized, like the rose quartz, geodes cracked open to reveal their hidden interior beauty, and a tiny piece of amber.

And then there were the figurines, a solid white virgin Mary sat next to an iron cross and a carved wooden Jesus. There were other things, a tiny bronze Buddha, a sage bundle, and leaning against the wall, a tiny canvas painting.

"Ahh!" I jumped back at the sight of it. Then I couldn't resist leaning in for a closer look, "What's that?"

She laughed, "That's Kali."

Kali's massive, bright red tongue stuck out. Her intense black eyes stared back with ire. She held a bloody sword as she kneeled over the body of her victim. "Shit. That's absolutely, horrible. Why do you have this?"

Molly smiled serenely as she also took in the image, "She's ferocious, isn't she? She protects the innocent and fights against evil. Or better still, she destroys darkness and changes it back into light."

"How does this not creep you out? It's the stuff of nightmares."

"Oh, Hal. You've been conditioned to see angels with white wings and glowing halos of light. But the truth is, angels aren't wilting violets, they wear combat boots."

Angels wear combat boots. Yet another, Mollyism, that I would never be able to shake from my brain.

Who was this woman?

She was as soft and sweet as summer rain falling on a tin roof. The kind of person who seemed as if she wouldn't hurt a living, breathing thing. Did her gentle nature cause people to underestimate her?

Maybe, she was really a warrior herself, transforming whenever the situation called for it.

"You are a different kind of person, aren't you?"

Molly looked uncomfortable and I worried that I might have offended her.

But then she said, "I'm a medium, Hal. For whatever reason, I was made this way so that I can help people. I've come to terms with the fact that I will never truly fit in."

"When I say, you are different, it's not meant as a judgement of right or wrong. It's more that you surprise me. I see the world differently when I'm around you."

"You're not scared of me?" she asked.

I shook my head, "Not at all. I think you make everything brighter. I feel better when I'm around you, hopeful even. I like you, Molly. I like you a lot."

She rolled her eyes, "Golly gee. Talk about turning on the charm. You must need a BIG favor, Mr. Winston."

"That is not why I said that, but yes, I do need a favor. Will you come?"

I had meant it, every word of it. I liked her.

So much so, that she infiltrated my thoughts day and night. Frankly, I was in awe of her, that she was so strong in who she was, so comfortable in her own skin, that she embraced all the strange differences about herself, unapologetically.

I think I might have even envied that she knew what it was that she was meant to do in this world.

She glanced at the clock on the wall, "Oh gosh, I have a zoom call with a client in a few minutes. I really do need to go and prepare for that. But yes, I'll come over. I should be available after say, 8:30?"

"Come whenever you can. In case Mamma is asleep, it's probably best not to knock. Just let yourself in."

She walked with me to the door. "Right. Until then. Have a good day, Hal."

I lingered for a lot longer than I needed to. It was hard for me to drag myself away and I wasn't sure how to say goodbye.

Should I hug her? I wanted to. Shake her hand? That seemed far too formal for our stage of knowing one another.

I settled on a simple thumbs up, "Thanks. You too." And awkwardly walked away.

I felt like my teenage self, the one who hadn't been brave enough to go in for the good night kiss. Had I really wanted in that moment, to kiss Molly?

Shut your whore mouth, Hal. You are not doing that to Sandy. Stop this, right now.

Mamma was still napping when I got back. I knew I should take advantage of this time to catch up on my own sleep. With all of the interruptions during the night, the periods when she woke me up for hours on end before settling back down again, it was hard to quantify how much sleep I'd gotten.

Only, I was too excited to sleep. Instead, I put in a grocery order for deliver. I wished that I'd asked Molly what kind of beer she liked. I ordered several different kinds, including a stout.

Because I'd slacked off on the housekeeping, it was beginning to look as if we'd been ransacked. I couldn't have Molly over with things this way, so I did a bit of cleaning too.

By the time I'd done all of this, my window for a nap had shut. The grocery deliver came, then Janine, then it was time to give Mamma her medications, and on and on, infinity.

Nancy arrived later than usual because of an emergency with a patient who lived in another county, almost forty minutes away. She looked tired.

I offered her a cup of coffee and was surprised when she actually accepted it. This was the first time she'd ever done so.

"It's been a day. One of our nurses is out sick and let's just say that everything that could have gone wrong, has. If I wasn't on the clock, I'd have a nice stiff drink."

"Believe me, I understand. If you weren't on the clock, I'd offer you one. It's the nature of all of this, isn't it?" I made a wide gesture with my hands to represent the capsulation of the entire bubble that I was in and its ever evolving, unpredictable changes.

"Sadly, yes. But speaking on the difficulty of your situation, I almost forgot. Rich should be contacting you tomorrow. Turns out your girlfriend got a senator interested in your situation. He made a few calls and yada, yada, yada. There is a facility that is going to accommodate the respite care for Ms. Rita."

"Are you serious? That's fucking fantastic! Sorry for cursing at you, but I'm just so happy. I think I might actually cry."

"I'll forgive that if you can forgive me for saying that you look like a zombie, Hal. I am more than a little concerned about your wellbeing. I was actually surprised to find out that you have a girlfriend. Not very hands on, is she?"

Nancy, flat out, was not afraid of saying whatever was on her mind, even at the risk of offending. It was simultaneously, refreshing and brutal.

Sandy was not here. She was not visibly supporting me. But she was helping. I felt bad because I had not even checked the recent messages that she'd left for me.

"This sort of thing is not in Sandy's wheel-house."

Nancy scowled at this, "Funny, I always thought having a partner meant having someone who had your back, no matter what. Don't get me wrong, what she did was nice and all, but it doesn't measure up to the kind of support you really need. I like you, Hal. I respect you for what you are doing here. You deserve a whole lot more than that."

"Halby. HALBY!!!!"

Nancy jumped so high, her coffee actually sloshed up out of her cup and then fell back inside again, "Dear Lord. Is there an axe murderer in there with her?"

"Nope. That's just the way she calls for me."

"Let's work on getting her a bell or something before somebody has a heart attack around here," Nancy moved quickly down the hall with me following, and peaked into the room. "Is it okay for me to come in? I wasn't sure with that distress call you sent out."

Mamma had taken off her oxygen and there was a slight tinge of blue to her lips, "I'm feeling very anxious right now."

Nancy retrieved the cannula from within the tangled-up bedsheet and invisibly slid it back into place, "Probably, because you weren't getting enough oxygen. I was going to put in a new catheter today, but it might be better just to wait until tomorrow."

She placed the pulse oximeter on Mamma's finger, "It's at 90, not too bad." Then she pulled out a blood pressure cuff and fastened the Velcro around her arm, "It's a little high, but nothing really concerning."

Nancy looked over the chart where I had written down the medications that I'd given, "Let's give her one of her pills for anxiety. That should help."

Her manner with my mother today was different. She wasn't as talkative as she usually was. She eyed Mamma in relative silence, listening to her chest and checking her over.

It was as if she could feel something was not quite right, even though she couldn't discern what that something was.

Before Nancy left, I asked, "What's wrong?"

She sighed and shifted the strap of her pink, vinyl bag, patterned with repeating caducei, syringes and traditional nurses' caps, on her shoulder, "I just have a feeling, but then I could be letting the day I've had, color my lens. You have my cell number. Don't hesitate to call if you need me."

I considered calling off drinks with Molly later. Nancy's heightened awareness, paired with my mother's refusal to eat anything, had me on edge.

Something, that I couldn't touch or see, was coming. Something I wasn't going to like very much. But then, one couldn't put everything on hold because of a feeling, either.

At 8:38 pm, Molly quietly closed the screen door behind her. She had on a knee length, indigo dress, a black cardigan and delicate looking, silver flip flops.

She'd fastened the top portion of her hair back, away from her face, making her look like a high school senior. And she wore the slightest hint of makeup.

It dawned on me that all the times before when I'd seen her, she hadn't been wearing any. It was a dramatic and stunning transformation. To be honest, I was a little rattled by it.

"I'm glad you could make it. Wow. It's a little warm in here. Is it warm to you? How was your day? I wasn't sure what kind of beer you liked. So, I bought all of them."

She giggled, "Let's see. Where do I start? It doesn't feel warm to me. I had a productive day. And I like any type of dark beer."

"Stout?" I asked.

"That works."

She followed me into the kitchen. I popped the top off of one of the beers and handed it to her.

She took a sip, closed her eyes, and said, "Oh, this is nice." Then she stared at my chin, "You shaved off your beard."

After showering, I'd taken a good long look at myself in the mirror. I looked much older than when I began this impromptu journey. I even had a couple of silver hairs that had sprung up out of nowhere.

"I decided that the ZZ Top look wasn't doing me any favors."

As soon as the deed was done, I'd gazed down at the pile of hair in the sink and had strong remorse over the decision. I missed it. My face felt too light, almost like I'd removed a layer of protection that I needed, somehow.

"I'm not going to lie. I have mixed feelings about the loss of the beard."

"I like being able to see your face." Molly smiled, took another swig from her beer, and asked, "How was your day?"

"You know that feeling, like when you go on a trip and the whole entire time that you're away, you're afraid that you forgot to do something really important. I've had that, almost the entire day."

"It sounds like you are having a premonition about something."

"I highly doubt that's the case." Even as I said it, though, I realized that what Molly said, summed this feeling up perfectly.

And I could tell from the look on Molly's face that she knew she'd hit a bullseye. "There are some theories that support non-linear time. If time isn't linear, then the future already exists, and you already know it. This makes the feeling that you are having, inevitable. Every single person on the planet experiences this in some way, at some time. It also means everyone is psychic to a certain degree."

"Good golly, Miss Molly. You're like some kind of oracle. That actually made sense to me."

I took a quick sip of my craft beer and asked, "So did you get a premonition about why I invited you over tonight?"

"Your question puts me in an awkward position."

"How so?"

Her face became guarded for several seconds before she released a long, slow breath, "Do I tell you everything I know which might make you feel too exposed? Do I tell you a little bit of what I see which might make you feel like I am in fact an oracle, but not in a scary way? Or do I lie to protect you and say absolutely nothing about what I know?"

"I'm not easily scared. Have you met my mother? Bring it on, sister."

"Ok. You have a question, information you need to retrieve from the spirit world and you are willing to explore my skill set, a skill that you definitely do not trust, to get it. You feel isolated and unsupported, but also that I am one of the few people around who can relate to what you are going through, and you feel safe talking to me. You are attracted to me, but you feel guilty about it, so you push these feelings down. But all you really wanted to do today when you said goodbye to me, was to kiss me."

I picked my jaw up from the floor, "Yep. That about sums it all up."

Molly sat her bottle of beer down on the kitchen counter, as if expecting that I might be on the verge of tossing her, head first, out the back door.

Her eyes rested on her lavender toenail polish, "Would you like for me to go?"

I placed my fingers gently under her chin and lifted her face up so that I could see into the depths of her sapphire eyes, "That is the last thing I need for you to do, Molly Owens."

The seconds stretched out as we remained locked into this unwavering gaze. It felt vast and infinite, like we'd fallen into a waking dream.

Molly was the first to recover and break the spell, "What did you need help with?"

I cleared my throat and swept away the cobwebs from my eyes, "There is a trust. The man who set it up for my mother is dead and I have no idea who he was to her, or why he did this for her. I was hoping you could ask him. I would pay you, of course."

She looked at me with pure annoyance, "I don't want money from you, Hal. There's a saying, you can't see the hurricane when you're standing in its eye. But I'm not inside of it. I can see. And it's a monster, Hal. It's gonna' snap off your arms and use them for toothpicks if you don't learn to accept help from other people."

I was pretty sure nobody else in the history of the world had ever said those exact words to anyone before, "That's a unique take on things. You think that if I keep shutting people out, that it won't end well for me?"

"Duh! That's what I just said." Molly picked up her beer, took a sip, and asked, "Was the man, who set it up, named, Joe?"

"Joe? No. Who's Joe?"

The first time I'd ever seen Molly, she'd been on the street talking to what my mother believed was the spirit of my dead father, which was ridiculous. But I was pretty sure she'd called someone by that name.

Molly blew a breath out through closed lips, causing them to vibrate with a soft puttering sound. She opened her mouth to answer, but before she could utter a single word, there was a sudden reality shift.

It came in the form of a gurgling, choking sound from my mother's bedroom.

CHAPTER SEVENTEEN

We found Mamma with her head resting against the stainless-steel bedrail. Her eyes were wide with panic, her chin and cannula coated in the same vomit that was puddled on her sheet and that dripped onto the floor.

I rushed in to sit her up. The air was heavy, foul and sour. I began to carefully roll up the mess inside of the linens.

"Here," Molly was suddenly there, holding a garbage can she'd grabbed from the bathroom, beneath my mother's chin.

"Thanks. Listen, you don't have to do that. This is a lot to deal with."

I reached for it, but Molly popped my hand and shot me a look that was both fierce and defiantly adorable, daring me to just try and take it from her.

I backed away, embarrassed, but not sure what else to do.

When Molly ignored me and began to gently stroke my mother's hair, I decided arguing was futile and simply let it be.

The moment I'd cleaned up the mess on the floor, the floodgates opened again. My mother violently, retched, until eventually, only dry heaves came. For what seemed like an eternity, she coughed and gagged in misery. But after a while, she relaxed, falling back with a sigh of exhaustion.

I'm not sure when Molly took away the dirty sheets and returned with clean ones. I didn't argue when she began to remove my mother's soiled nightgown.

I allowed this.

I watched her gently lift Mamma's arms and slip it off, and I felt such gratitude for Molly. I was grateful for her quick thinking, for her not being disgusted by it all, and for her being here.

I was grateful that she had refused to leave me alone. Just her being here, had made this horrible thing that was happening, not feel so overwhelming.

If this had actually been a first date, it would have gone down in the record books as the worst date ever.

Molly took the tub Janine used for my mother's baths and filled it with warm water. Then with a washcloth and foamy soap, she began to gingerly wash away the whole event.

My first instinct was to take over, but something stopped me. I surrendered to flow of the moment without trying to insert my will over it or control it.

Molly dried her off with a towel, dressed her in a clean gown, and began brushing the tangles out of her hair.

Mamma eyed Molly with a serene curiosity, relaxing more with each brushstroke. But then she put her hand on Molly's arm and said, "I misjudged you. I'm sorry for thinking you were a witch."

Molly patted her hand and with perfect comedic timing, said, "That alright. I'm sorry for thinking you were a bitch."

My mother chuckled. And just like that, Molly was seamlessly absorbed into our bubble.

She was absorbed in a way that only a certain kind of person could have been, the best kind of person, the strangest and most wonderful kind, who was filled with so much love they couldn't hold anything else in their hearts other than kindness and forgiveness.

By 11:00 pm, things were settled enough for me to text Nancy.

Guess what? I know what your weird feeling was about. Mamma has had a rough night. Vomiting a lot. No fever though. But I think we are through the worst of it.

She texted back right away.

I'm glad you let me know. She's been heavy on my mind. I will be there first thing in the morning to check on her. Try to get some rest, Hal.

Molly had dozed off in the recliner. I leaned over her and softly whispered, "Wake up, sleepy head."

She yawned, opening her eyes slowly as if it took great will power to do so. Then she sat up and squinted at the small digital clock on the nightstand. "I should go. Will you be alright?"

"I'll be fine. I don't know how to repay you for what you did for us. It went above and beyond."

"Don't, Hal. It wasn't an accident that I was here tonight. I was placed here to do this for you."

She said this matter-of-factly, as though this was just the way things were, like what had happened was a completely normal occurrence.

I'd invited her over tonight to solve a completely different problem. My conditioning wanted to frame it as a fortunate coincidence that Molly had been here to help, and that's all.

But if I looked at things with the theory Molly had shared with me about time in mind, I had asked her over on this particular night because I already knew that I was going to need her.

I already knew that she would give me a hard time about not being open to receiving help. I already knew that it would all work out, because I'd already seen it.

I'd sensed it coming, the same way that Nancy had.

Was this God? Was he the almighty keeper of time? Was he the magician behind the curtain manipulating matter the way a child worked playdough on a kitchen table?

I wasn't sure what to say after Molly rebuked the thank you that I'd extended. But I needed her to know how much it had meant to me. "I wish you would just accept my extreme and heart felt gratitude without arguing with me."

At once, Molly seemed to understand this and relented, "You're welcome, Hal."

There was a rumble of thunder. The rain began to fall as soon as she stepped onto the street. It was the first in weeks, falling in large, heavy droplets that instantly soaked Molly's hair and dress.

But she didn't run like mad to get out of it like any old ordinary person would have. She stopped in her tracks and lifted up her face to meet it.

With her mouth open, she let it wash over her. And when she eventually made her way toward her house, she did so in a slow, thoughtful way.

It was like being out in this deluge, was something that she savored, a cherished favorite thing she had not done in a very long time.

It might have been then when I realized there was a strong possibility that I was in love with her.

CHAPTER EIGHTEEN

Rich called early to deliver the good news. A facility, half an hour away, was prepared to accommodate my mother's respite care in two days' time.

This meant I had a lot to do to get ready, such as deciding what things needed to be packed for her and coordinating with the people who would facilitate this. But also, I needed to plan how I would make the most of my five days off.

Nancy was with me during this call. As soon as I'd hung up, she said, "It's about freaking time you get a break." She was also on a call, with a person who was bringing an X-ray machine to get images of my mother's lungs.

But somehow the technician had gotten turned around in an area where GPS didn't work and was having to rely on her directions to reach us.

When the six-foot-two linebacker of a man, dressed in blue scrubs, arrived and rolled in the large machine, Mamma reacted fearfully, "What are you doing? I don't want that thing in here." Her pale grey eyes darted back and forth between man and machine. It wasn't clear which of them was scaring her most.

"They need to take an image of your lungs. That's what the machine is for," Nancy said.

"NO! He's going to hurt me."

"Mamma, nobody is going to hurt you. They need to do this to make sure that everything is okay." I stood at her side and placed my hand on her arm, reassuringly.

This seemed to calm her down. That was until the man attempted to slide the panel of film behind her back and all hell swiftly broke loose.

Mamma caught his arm with her nails, managing to open a long gash that instantly filled with blood, "Get away from me. HELP! He's trying to murder me!"

The technician drew back with unveiled exasperation and Nancy handed him an alcohol swab and a bandage for his battle wound. It was clear that he had one foot out the door unless something changed quickly.

"I'm really sorry about that," I said, trying to smooth over the fallout that was caused by intergenerational meanness.

He shrugged, as if to say, let it go. The hulk of a man cleaned his hands with sanitizer before donning a new pair of gloves that struggled to fit him.

Nancy moved to the opposite side of the bed, "Listen Rita, you are safe. Do you think I would let anybody hurt you?"

Mamma looked at her as if she had just stated the most stupidly obvious thing possible, "I know that, Nancy. But you don't know anything about this person. *He* might want to hurt me. And he brought that machine that is going to give me cancer."

Nancy took the film panel from the technician and said, "No, ma'am. Nobody is giving anybody cancer on my watch." Then she effortlessly, maneuvered Mamma forward and slid the panel behind her, "Close your eyes, Ms. Rita. Don't open them until I tell you to."

To my complete amazement, my mother did what Nancy asked of her. In just a few seconds, the image was taken, and the disgruntled giant wheeled the feared machine away.

"You can open your eyes now," Nancy said.

Mamma searched the room in such a meticulous and melodramatic manner, I thought she was going to have us check underneath the bed to make sure there was nobody hiding there.

"That wasn't so bad, was it?" I asked.

The X-ray revealed that my mother still had pneumonia. Nancy ordered another round of antibiotics for her. And I began easing Mamma into the idea of temporarily going into a facility.

"Will I be there long?" she asked.

"Only five days. Then they will bring you back home."

"Are you going to be here when I get back?" Tears rolled from the corners of her eyes.

I grabbed a tissue, wiped them away, and handed it to her. "Of course, I will. I just need some time to take care of a few personal things." This was true. I hadn't been to my store in months. And it hadn't seemed right to tell her that I needed a vacation from her.

"You know that might be for the best. You're not looking so good, Halby."

"Gee, thanks, Mamma."

"It isn't easy taking care of me, is it?"

"No, it is not. But that's OK. I'm happy to do it."

"Can you ever forgive me?" she asked.

What she was asking forgiveness for?

Was it for the years of abuse I'd been subjected to? Was it for the years wasted because neither of us had been able to escape our own woundedness?

Or was she simply, sorry because I had been working so hard on her behalf? Because this woman had been given the blessing of forgetting a painful past.

I let myself believe that it was all of these things, that buried in her subconscious, there was a part of her that needed this and wanted to heal the wrongs between us.

"I have already forgiven you, for everything. We are right as rain, Mamma."

She grabbed my hand and drew me down, until my face was near her own and I could see the blueness of veins underneath the ashen paler of her skin. Then she softly, touched her lips to my cheek.

This time I didn't bother to hold back the floodgate. I wept, gut wrenching cries pouring out of me, my face pressed into her shoulder.

At some point, I noticed a hand patting me on the back, comforting me. And then I heard her words, thin wispy things, hanging in the air. I barely caught them, "I love you. It's all going to be alright."

"I love you too, Rita Winston."

And then she surprised me, pulling me out of my sadness by asking, "When I come home, can we release the Chinese lanterns again?"

I wiped my face and chuckled. "How many would you like?"

"Not too many, maybe just a hundred."

"*One hundred?* Sure. Why not?"

We were definitely going to bring the entirety of the Hollow Oaks Neighborhood down in flames.

I called Sandy's number and waited. She picked up after the second ring, "Hal! Shit! I'm glad it's you. So, the respite care is happening, then?"

This was my chance to come clean about my feelings, to own up to everything that I'd been hiding from her, "Yes, in a couple of days. Thank you for fighting for that, Sandy. None of this has been fair to you. I've left you hanging in limbo and I'm sorry for that."

"Don't apologize. I understand."

"No, I don't think you do. This whole experience has taken more out of me than I ever could have imagined. I haven't known how to even talk to you about what's happening here, or how hard it's been. I've declined physically. I look like a fucking scarecrow. I hardly sleep. I'm nearly bankrupt. But it's changed me, Sandy. In ways that I would have never expected."

"Oh, Hal. We'll get that turned around. I can give you some money to tide you over until you can get your business up and going. Don't worry about that."

"That's the thing. I want to be honest with myself. I haven't been. Not for a long, long time. My business has barely been making it, for a while now. And I just kept holding onto it, because to let it go meant that I had failed, because it was my entire world, this haven I created to hide inside of. But I don't want to do that anymore. I want to let it go and reach for something else."

"Hal, you're not a failure because you want to do something new. People do that all the time. It's not your fault that electronics repair is becoming obsolete."

"It's a little more than that, though. I repaired things because I didn't know how to repair myself. It was predictable and safe because I couldn't cope with anything that wasn't. Kind of like us."

A long silence stretched out. It was a punch in the gut to Sandy. I could feel it. And she was grappling with it all. "Are you telling me you want us to take a break?"

"Sandy, I care about you deeply. I always will. But I don't think we are the right people for one another. I think you know that too."

"Wow! This was not what I was expecting to happen today. I feel completely blindsided."

"I don't want to hurt you. It pains me deeply that this will hurt you. But I am not the Hal you knew, Sandy. He's gone. And no amount of necromancy can bring him back."

"I don't want to lose you." Her voice was foreign, raw with uncharacteristic emotion.

It dawned on me that she was silently crying. I had never even seen her cry before.

"Hey. I'm still here for you. We don't have to suddenly start hating each other, do we?"

"I don't know how I feel at the moment. I might hate you. But I also, may not hate you. I think I'll need to sleep on it."

"But we will always have Siracha sauce, right?"

She laughed and blew her nose, "You're an idiot."

It was because of her that I had learned that popcorn was just not the same without it. I would never be able to go into another theatre to watch a movie without smuggling a bottle of the stuff in.

Sandy definitely regretted introducing this concept to me.

"I certainly won't miss the weird stares we got on movie nights," she said.

"If it would make you feel better, I could compose a list of all the annoying things about me and email it to you."

"Thank you, but I think I can handle that list just fine on my own. Goodbye, Hal. Take care of yourself."

"You too, Sandy."

I sat in a sort of shocked silence. I wasn't even sure how I felt about this part of my life ending.

A few months ago, if you had told me that my life was going to implode, that I would soon be teetering on the verge of financial ruin, I would have thought you were off the chain, touched in the head, and in need of your very own padded room.

Because that Hal, thought he had it all figured out and that his life was perfectly fine the way it was. That Hal, hadn't been able to conceive of anything that could possibly come in to change that.

This had been neither a gentle nor vindictive redirection by the universe. One could even say that it had been done out of kindness, forcing the change that was needed in order for me to grow and really see how off course I'd gone in my life.

I felt as if what I'd really been given, was a second chance and the wisdom to see it that way.

There was a reason we couldn't see too far into the future. Because if we could, we would pack our bags and drive over a cliff. We'd throw in our towels because the prospect of what we had to face would be too much to bear. But that was not the point.

The point was what we learned in the gaps, not when things were going according to our plans, not within the actual shit show that disrupted them, but in the calm that preceded and in the quiet that followed.

In these moments of clarity something beautiful was revealed to us. We understood what was really important. For most of us, going through truly unbearable things was the only way we could ever hope to catch a glimpse of it.

All I knew was that today, things were precisely the way they needed to be.

CHAPTER NINETEEN

I had turned my phone to silent mode the previous evening and hadn't remembered to turn it back on until after I'd watched my mother being wheeled away.

I'd missed a call and there was a voice message.

I instantly recognized the number for Chandley & Stewart.

Hello, Mr. Winston. This is Tracy calling back about the matter concerning your mother. If you could, please give me a call at you earliest convenience, I will be here today until 6:00pm.

I wondered if anyone would be in the office at 7:00 am. A young male answered.

"This is Hal Winston, returning a call from Tracy."

A minute later, I heard Tracy's sweet and well-modulated, Southern accent, "Hello. I wanted to let you know that I was able to track down someone here who has knowledge of your mother's trust, but he won't speak with you over the phone. We would need to schedule an appointment for you to come in and meet in person."

I explained my situation and the narrow window that I had available to handle this. Tracy checked the calendar to see what time slots were available, "I'm afraid Mr. Howard is booked pretty solid during those days. Oh wait, there is one time, but it might not be convenient since you are traveling so far."

It was at 8:00 am. That would mean getting up super early and sacrificing much needed sleep, but I didn't see what other choice I had. "I'll take it. Thank you, for your help with this. I really do appreciate it."

"No problem at all. We'll see you then." Tracy gave me the address, instructions about where to park, and suggestions for hotels that were nearby should I decide to go that route.

The timing of this was uncanny. It felt like it had all been orchestrated behind the scenes by some unseen force. And it made me think about what Molly had said about nothing being coincidental.

After the call, I sat on the sofa in a tangle of thoughts and feelings. I decided that it was possible to climb out of the crumbling pillars of my life to lay down a new foundation. Today, that felt daunting, like I wouldn't be able to muster the strength to do it.

Maybe it all came down to just having faith, taking one small step toward something and believing that it would someday work out and make sense to me.

Maybe it was a fake it until you make it, scenario, ignoring the fear of change and taking action without delay.

In these past months, I'd learned a thing or two about the high cost of wasted time. And at the end of my life, I didn't want to be steeped in regret.

I wanted to be living in the dream I'd had, happy, in a hammock on the beach, with Molly Owens showering me with sweet, honeysuckle flavored kisses.

It was too early to be on Molly's doorstep.

I had not really been expecting her to answer the door at this early hour, especially not dressed in a long floral robe, makeup free, with tousled honey blonde hair, and still looking so lovely.

"Hey. I was asleep. Is something wrong?"

"No! I'm sorry. I didn't mean to wake you up. They took Mamma to a facility for few days. And I'm heading back to Knoxville to take care of some personal matters,"

"Thank you for keeping me updated. Would you like to come in? I could make some coffee."

All I wanted to do was to scoop her up in my arms and kiss her feverishly, but I also knew that was not how I wanted our story to begin.

If Molly would have anything to do with me, I wanted it to be a bigger, deeper love story, that began with so much more than a gratuitous pleasure grab.

"I should probably get going. But I needed to say something. I like you, Molly Owens. I really, really, do."

"I like you too, Hal."

"No, it's more than that. I think I might be in love with you. And that's weird, because we don't know each other very well and I don't want to scare you away. When I'm with you, I feel like anything is possible. I feel like everything in my life was just leading me to you."

I paused and waited for her to say something. I waited for her to tell me that I was way out of line, here. Her face was serene, and I wasn't sure, but it looked like the hint of a smile was forming at the corners of her lips.

This gave me courage to continue, "Today, I'm officially closing out an old cycle in my life. And I was wondering if you might be…if you might be interested in starting something new with me, Molly?"

Molly considered me with eyes that were as vast and as blue as the Mediterranean Sea, "Could we maybe discuss this over, say, dinner?"

I grinned, encouraged by the fact that she hadn't slammed the door in my face or called the cops on me, "That would work. Can I call you when I get back?"

Suddenly, her hint of a smile shapeshifted into a slightly demure one. It caused my pulse to accelerate wildly.

"You can call me," she said.

"Good. Perfect." I turned to go, deciding it would be better to take this win and dash away with it as quickly as possible, before she decided I was an utter lunatic and changed her mind.

But Molly wasn't ready to let me leave yet, "Wait! You didn't let me finish. I would like to start something new with you, Hal Winston. I would like that very much."

A disconnect grew between what I had planned to do and what I really wanted to do, what I'd wanted to do almost from the first time I'd met Molly.

I drew her into my arms and pressed my lips against hers.

It was the sweetest sort of kiss. She yielded against me, tasting like honeysuckle that had been sitting in full sun all day long and of vanilla lip balm.

I pulled away in time to note the dreamy expression on her face.

"How long will you be gone?" she asked.

I smoothed back a section of hair that had landed across in her right eye, "A couple of days, maybe."

"Get some rest, will you?"

I chuckled, "Yes, ma'am. Next time you see me, I might not have the dark circles underneath my eyes."

"I'm pretty sure I'll be just fine with that. Be kind to yourself, Hal."

Leave it to Molly to accurately, assess the right thing to say. It was like she knew that what I was going to do might leave me vulnerable to falling into despair and nostalgia over what was being left behind.

Now, I would have her voice in my head, reminding me to treat myself with the same compassion that I would extend to anyone else who happened to be down on their luck or going through hard times.

I knew this advice would help to see me to the other side of it.

Mr. Fabiano threw his arms out when I walked into his office. His hands always told half of the story, "Hal! You're back. People have been asking about you."

I knew that he was part Greek and part Italian. He had never volunteered much more than that and I had never asked. I was certain that he sat behind his desk so much to hide the fact that he was not a tall man.

"You look BAD, Hal. Really, bad. How's your mother?"

"Not so good, I'm afraid. I wanted to talk to you about that."

I laid a copy of my bank statement down on his desk for him to see. He glanced at it in surprise and then looked away with a pained expression, "Why you show me this? That's not good."

"I know that I have seven months left on the lease, but I was hoping we could come to some sort of agreement. I came back to officially close up the store.

He leaned back in his chair and folded his arms across his chest. I could actually see the cogs in his brain turning and working out what he considered to be a fair solution.

"Hal, I am truly, sorry. You have been a good tenant. Never given me any problems. Pay me for two months. That will give me time to find someone else to take over the space. And if I get someone in sooner than that, I will return your money."

I nodded, "Thank you. That's more than fair. I wasn't planning on taking any of the furniture in the apartment. That might be a plus for someone."

Mr. Fabiano pondered this, "That will work. Just leave it clean. Only the furniture, okay? Not a bunch of crap I got to clean out."

I gave him a thumbs up, "Got it. No crap!" I wrote out a check and handed it over to him before picking up my statement. "I'll drop the keys off when I'm done."

I walked two doors down and unlocked the door. With the lights on, the spiders that had overtaken things, scurried into hiding. I grabbed a broom and began clearing away cobwebs and reclaiming the space.

There were boxes overflowing with spare parts, circuit boards, fuses, various sized bolts and screws, and wires, lots and lots of wires that I painstakingly went through.

Some items I knew I could easily sell online. That was good and would generate temporary income. Most of it, anything I didn't think I could make money from, got tossed into the dumpster out back.

I called a warehouse down the street that specialized in used office equipment. A guy ran right over and offered me a thousand dollars for the old cash register, display cases, shelves, and everything else that he decided he would be able to resale.

It didn't bother me that I could have gotten more for all of these things if I had sold them on my own. I simply didn't have the time to do it. The part of me that would have been preoccupied with this before, wasn't.

There was this strong feeling that I wasn't really losing anything, that what I was gaining by letting it all go, would more than make up for it.

And when I got bogged down in self-doubt and regrets about wasting so many years here, or thinking I hadn't really accomplished anything—I did what Molly had told me to do.

I was kind to that past Hal. I told him that he had saved lots of people money by fixing their old things in a way that would last them another ten years or more.

I told him that he had saved the environment by preventing those old things from ending up in landfills.

I told him that he had been quietly healing himself that entire time, he just hadn't known it.

I told him that his life before had been necessary to lead him into this new one, and that this next phase of it, lurking beyond his awareness, would make him grateful for all of it.

He only needed to have faith.

It was nearly midnight. I took in the cream-colored walls, stripped bare of posters and signs. The white and emerald green, checker board, linoleum tile had been mopped clean.

It was only a shell, full of potential, same as the first day I'd first found this place. It was a clean slate for the next dreamer with an idea of how to carve out a living within these walls.

The neon sign in the window, I would take down tomorrow. That would go with me, a token to help me remember how stark the before, had really been.

I turned off the lights and headed upstairs, where I opened up the window that faced out toward the alleyway and climbed out onto the fire escape.

The sounds from the downtown street drifted up to meet me. My view, directly across, was the brick wall of a Japanese restaurant.

A few cars had parked below in spite of signs warning that all vehicles would be towed. They almost never were. And I could see people hurrying along the sidewalk on their way to the only bar that was still open, unaware of eyes watching them from above.

When I was younger, I had loved the novelty of a loft downtown and the convenience of living above my business.

Tonight, I missed looking out into the limbs of trees and hearing the rustling of their leaves in the wind. I missed the grass that when I left, was up to my knees. And I missed the quiet, not having traffic horns blaring and that the only person shouting out at all hours of the night, was my mother.

But most of all, I missed Molly, and her being only a short walk away.

I thought about the new life I wanted, what it would look like, smell like, taste like. That's where my focus settled, until I lay my head down and fell asleep.

CHAPTER TWENTY

I opened my eyes at 5:00 am, disoriented and hungry. My first instinct was to run in to check on Mamma. But then I noticed the gold damask curtain hanging and remembered that I was back in Knoxville.

All these years of waking up, staring at it, and thinking, I should install a real closet door before Sandy could give me a hard time about it, again.

And all this time, I never had.

The innards of my refrigerator looked like a bio weapons lab, moldy potatoes, lunch meat that had developed some sort of luminescent slime on its surface.

There was a slice of pizza that looked suspiciously unchanged, preserved in a way that tempted me to just nuke it and bite in anyway.

Had my time in the bubble turned me into the type of person who would eat three-month old pizza? Or had it made me fearless enough to try it?

I definitely wasn't ready to die from food poisoning, not after I'd committed to going full throttle in the direction of change.

Instead, I toasted an entire package of waffles that were in the freezer, smothering them in butter and powdered sugar, and washed them down in record time with a cup of chicory coffee.

With my hunger contained, I ended the science experiment, emptying everything from the refrigerator and pantry into a garbage bag and throwing it down two stories, into the dumpster.

Clothes were sorted through and separated into piles, things for donation and things that would go with me. Until at some point, it became so tedious, I decided I would only take the things I actually wore and liked, and stuffed them inside a giant suitcase.

The unit got a thorough cleaning. Photographs were taken down from the wall. A mass of wires was untangled from the phonograph and speakers, and albums were packed into milk crates to take to my mother's house.

Blankets, sheets, and knickknacks got tossed into the boxes to be given to charity.

There was little that I wanted to keep. I guessed, in my soul, I had always been a minimalist. Over time, the weight of the things I'd accumulated had unbeknownst to me, begun to anchor me more and more to this loft apartment I had thought of as home.

I was surprised to find that saying goodbye to it, wasn't that hard. In fact, it felt good. I felt lighter than I could remember being in a long time.

I had dismantled it all, scrubbed everything to sparkling, and when I stood back to survey the results of hours and hours of labor, thought it looked better this way, without the distraction of clutter, without the heaviness of possessions.

I considered inviting Sandy over to toast this transformation with a glass of wine. I wanted her to see it now, this space, we'd spent so many hours together in.

It could be a combination of both truce and closure.

I knew it was too soon for that. Letting go was not something that came easy to Sandy, and letting go on someone else's terms, was never easy for anyone.

Someday, I was positive she would look back and see our break-up as the best thing that had ever happened to her. She might even call me to brag about all the great things that had happened in her life since me, and really rub in how I'd passed up a good thing.

And she would be right. She was a good thing. She was fun and beautiful, brilliant and all kinds of fabulous. And I had freed her, I hoped, to find her soul mate.

I loaded up the Bronco and headed to a donation center. The sun was bright. It was warmer than average today, nearly seventy degrees, but somehow it still felt like fall.

Maybe it was the way the foliage had begun to change colors and wither. Maybe it was the pumpkin spice menu items at the café where I went to refuel with more coffee. But it made me long for bonfires and camping under the stars, something that I had not done in ions.

I drove through the UT campus, taking in historic brick buildings and students who looked so young, I couldn't believe I had ever been like them.

I was an entirely different person. All the cells that made up that Halbert Thomas Winston, had been replaced with new ones.

I was a man, the Hal of my past, would have considered old, a man he never thought he'd live long enough to become.

Why had I never thought I'd make it into my late thirties?

It probably stemmed from a fear that a genetic switch would get flipped and I would suddenly turn into my mother, personifying the darkest aspects of her personality or those of a father I knew nothing about, and that I'd end up drinking myself into an early grave.

Being in the bubble, had forced me sit with myself and look at things I had refused to face, like what had caused me to run away from a career in psychology.

Back then, I had believed that my difficult upbringing made me ill equipped to help others. But this line of thinking had been completely flawed.

My brushes with mental illness, unmet potential, and unhealed heartache, gave me a unique perspective on suffering. They gave me a depth of understanding I could have never obtained had I not lived the life that I had.

My experiences had a grander design. Everything had led me to this moment and readied me to be propelled, like a slingshot, back onto the right path, at exactly, the right time.

At the donation center, there was a carline with volunteers directing people through. When it was my turn, the young girl pulled out her walkie talkie and radioed for assistance with moving it all inside.

She handed over a receipt for when I filed my taxes and thanked me for generously giving back to the community.

I knew it was a canned response, but it sounded nice. In just a few seconds, a handful of people had removed everything, disappearing behind a heavy metal door with bits and pieces of my life.

To celebrate this momentous occasion, I drove to my favorite burger joint and treated myself to a plate with all the fixins. This I ate while sitting on the hood of my car, parked along the weedy banks of the Tennessee River, watching boat traffic drift by.

The world was vast. It used to feel too big and overwhelming to me. I was afraid of what I'd find if I ventured too far out into it.

But even this river branched out. It flowed into tributaries. It ran into creeks and channels, and network upon network of water systems that spanned great distances.

Most days, being in the bubble with my mother, felt like I was on the receiving end of terrible misfortune. It was a heavy burden that I had no way of escaping. But it had broken me free from the patterns of my life in a way that made the things I'd feared before, now seem very minor and small.

I knew that everything would be just fine.

I would be like this river. I wouldn't fight the flow of where life wanted to take me.

I would trust it to take me where I needed to be.

CHAPTER TWENTY-ONE

I was so tired that I could hardly stand up by the time I had finished with everything that needed to be done. I had scheduled for the power to be turned off and for the final bill to be mailed to my mother's address.

It was still dark out when I packed up the truck. I slid the keys into an envelope with a letter and pushed it through the mail slot.

The letter had been short and to the point.

Dear Mr. Fabiano,

Thank you for taking a chance on a clueless, young chap with absolutely no credit history. I am sorry for being late with rent that one time. It was truly because of the situation with my mother. I hope this doesn't stop you from finding the kindness within yourself to take a chance on the next twenty something who walks through your door with nothing but a dream and prayer.
Take care of yourself, you old curmudgeon.

Hal

When I drove away, I was way too focused on the things ahead of me to look back. I cued up a playlist I'd made sometime last year.

It was all over the place and included bands like, The Ramones, Roxy Music, Dionne Warwick, Abba, Radiohead, Red Hot Chili Peppers, and Nancy Griffith. It was a mixed-up bundle that matched, this weirdo, right here.

An orange glow filled the skyline, hinting of the inevitable rising of the sun. Molly would be in bed when I returned, but that was alright.

Before I let the fog of love completely, sidetrack me, I had to figure out where to order one hundred Chinese lanterns and find a place to put all the stuff I had crammed inside of the Bronco.

And I needed to cut the damn, grass.

Then I would plan out the most romantic dinner imaginable, one that was sure to win over hearts and minds, or just one heart and one mind.

I pulled onto I-40 and swore under my breath that there was so much traffic already. I contemplated pulling off and searching for an alternate route that would keep me away from all the congestion.

But then, *If Anybody Had a Heart*, came on and I forgot all about how annoyed I'd been, as I drank my fast-food coffee and ate my sausage and egg biscuit.

Yesterday, I'd called the facility to check on my mother. They told me that she had been bragging about having a son named, Halby, who cooked for her and took great care of her.

She also told them that I would be back to get her as soon as I got back from performing onstage at Radio City Music Hall with Elvis Presley and the Rockettes.

This was all news to me, of course. I mean, Elvis hadn't been on the radar since she and I had helped him out at Madison Square Garden. And for him to be performing with the Rockettes, who wouldn't want to find out what that was all about?

It was after seven when I pulled off toward Piney Valley, a lonely exit, with no restaurants or strip malls to prove it was not just some backwoods place, chock-full of hillbillies with guns.

It was the polar opposite of Knoxville, Tennessee.

I stopped at the end of the driveway to check the mail and realized that I was not battling overgrown weeds to do so.

Someone had cut them all back. And someone had also cut the grass, edged the sidewalk, and replenished the flower beds.

I wandered through the yard for a long time, taking it all in. Who could have done this?

At first, I thought it had to be Molly Owens. But then I found a note stuck inside the door from Nancy.

I just couldn't stand to look at this sad little yard for one more day.

I had tears in my eyes. It was such a sweet gesture that she would take time to do this for us. Only Nancy could both bring me to tears, but also, have me wondering if she could get away with talking to me in this way.

She would be pissed if she knew I hadn't been resting, and she wouldn't understand my urgency to get so many things done, immediately, if not sooner.

I had this weird feeling again, that something was going to happen, something I couldn't foresee, and that I needed to be prepared for it.

But then I shrugged it off, putting it down to acute fatigue and looked into ordering lanterns.

The state of Tennessee promptly put the nix to this idea. Turns out sky lanterns require a special license that I did not have.

I assumed this was because they didn't want them crashing back down and setting structures and the odd pet on fire.

Leave it to big government to spoil things for everyone. I would have to come up with some kind of compromise to appease Mamma. I knew between myself and Molly, we could figure something out.

I ordered groceries. Not sure what type of foods Molly liked, I ordered everything I could think of between the range of vegan and blood thirsty carnivore.

I selected some recipes in the different categories, just in case, but secretly, I hoped she would be happy with steaks, baked potatoes, and salad, something I couldn't screw up.

Although, I had grown to be a decent cook over the past few months. I discovered I kind of liked fooling around in the kitchen and creating things that would get the thumbs up or down from my mother. But I really didn't want to burn up a meal on our first official date.

I would definitely take a long nap. I would sleep without setting an alarm. I would let go of everything else and do that one thing to pamper myself.

And I made a promise. *Hal Winston, you are going to do a much better job going forward of taking care of yourself. You will ask for help when you need it, you will accept that help, and you will offer help when you can. You will not be an island anymore.*

I finished unloading the truck. All the boxes of things I planned to sell got locked in the shed. My clothes went into the closet in my old room.

My desk held a cup full of pens and florescent markers that I had placed there who knows when. There was the same red, white, and blue plaid quilt on the same twin bed I'd grown up sleeping in.

The only change that I observed was a charcoal sketch of a cabin my mother had hung above the bed.

To be honest, I'd mostly avoided this room, leaving the door closed and sleeping in the chair in my mother's room, or on the sofa in the living room.

And now, I had this sudden realization that she had wanted me to come home, maybe even expected me to. I wasn't sure how I felt about that.

Yes, I regretted the way it had been between us. But I didn't feel bad about setting boundaries between me and an abusive person. I would never let myself go there.

Had I come home and seen my framed note, kindly telling her to fuck off, I would have probably turned around and left again.

Without having actually told me that she loved me, she had.

She'd left my room almost like a time capsule, because she hadn't been able to let go of me and move on.

I had severed things in such a way that it had been like death, the death of what we were to one another, the death of our family. I was gone, unreachable, and she had silently and in her own way, grieved for me.

I sat down on the squeaky mattress that sat on top of even squeakier box springs. I let myself do what I had been afraid of doing this whole time. I released the floodgates. I ugly cried.

I sobbed like a toddler who had gotten a lump of coal on Christmas morning. And in doing so, I let go of all the disappointment, the hurt, the anger, the not feeling like I was good enough.

I forgave my mother for every horrible, shitty, evil thing she had ever done to hurt me. And then I thanked the powers above for giving me this time with Mamma, this chance to work on healing my broken heart.

I'd been looking at this situation with my mother as a curse. When all along, it had really been a blessing.

I fell back, laid my head against the pillow, and stared up at the ceiling. Then I began to laugh.

There was a poster of Alicia Silverstone still stapled there. How could I have forgotten how in love with that woman I had been? My dream of marrying her for sure had not come to fruition.

I closed my eyes and did something that would make Nancy very happy. I took a five-hour, uninterrupted, drool coming out of my mouth, nap.

CHAPTER TWENTY-TWO

Molly opened the door with a single finger held against her lips, indicating that I should be quiet. She smiled and pointed to one of the plush red chairs and I sat down without making a sound.

She took a seat on the sofa and arranged her computer on her lap, "Sorry, about that. No, I don't think that was something you should be frightened about. Ronald comes across as someone who liked to play tricks on people. Not to be mean, but to make people laugh."

Another woman's voice chimed in and I realized she was on a Zoom call, "Wow. Molly. I had forgotten about that. He totally got a kick out of being a trickster. Do you think he knocked the bag of flour off the counter just to make me laugh? Because I didn't laugh about it. I was fit to kill. And I was scared because the way it happened was so strange."

"I don't think he necessarily wanted to make you laugh. What he really wanted, was to get your attention. And he did, didn't he? If he had done something smaller, he knew you wouldn't have noticed it because you've been so distracted lately. He is showing me an image of you working and looking haggard, so he may be concerned about that. He might think you are staying too busy, and would like for you to take some time for yourself. He also showed me an image of a red car, kind of like an old British one, and then he showed me that it's in a garage under a tarp."

I could tell by the change in the woman's voice that she had begun to cry, "Yes. It sure is. A Triumph Spitfire. He loved that damn car. I can't even look at it because it just makes me think of him. And it's too painful."

"Maybe what he is trying to get across is that you are staying too busy as a way of not processing your emotions over his sudden death. And the car would be a good way for you to start, either by selling it or driving it. And the bag of flour and the other things you've been noticing since, are his way of showing you that he is never truly going to leave you."

The woman, on the call, cried for a long time while Molly sat patiently. Then she composed herself and blew her nose, "I want to apologize to you, Molly. When my friend recommended you, I didn't believe you were the real deal. I almost canceled today. But I was out in the rose garden and a white butterfly landed on my nose, and sat there for the longest time. It was so odd, I thought maybe I should just see what you had to say. But you've said so many things that nobody could have known about. But more than that. You've given me comfort."

I was sure Molly got that a lot, people doubting her. I listened for the rest of the conversation in complete awe of what transpired. I was convinced Molly was some kind of earth angel, sent here to ease the suffering of others by helping them work through difficult things.

The world was full of charlatans and scammers, people who would cheat you out of your last dime without the slightest hesitation or remorse about it.

They took, took, took until the well went dry, then they found a new sucker to leach off of. In other words, the opposite of Molly Owens, who gave, and gave, and gave, only her well never seemed to run dry.

It didn't matter what was happening around her, she was happy. She was grounded in self-belief. Molly had faith in herself even when others doubted her.

I guessed her kind of gentle power was hard for most people to understand.

As Molly ended her call and closed her laptop, I said, "That was amazing. You make people, happy. Is that like your super power?"

"They aren't always happy. Sometimes people don't like what I have to say, or aren't ready to hear the truth. In those cases, I like to think that I planted the seed, that maybe they will be ready to revisit later with or without me."

I motioned toward a diploma hanging on her wall from UT, "We have something in common, Molly. Psychology. I graduated with the same degree. As we speak, it's growing mold in a box in my mother's shed."

"All I'm doing here is combining what I've learned at an institution and the abilities I was given, to help others.

Have you ever thought it's time to take that diploma out of the shed and put it to use?"

"As a matter of fact, I have. I closed my store while I was gone. The world is my oyster now."

She grinned, "You don't say. That's kind of exciting, don't you think?"

It was interesting that she used the word, exciting, instead of telling me how sorry she was about this like other people would have.

But I was excited, excited when I should have been worried about how I was going to carve out a new living. I wasn't scared, not at all.

I just knew that everything would work out.

"I didn't mean to barge in and interrupt your work like this. I really just wanted to find out if you were free to come over for dinner tonight."

She came to me, leaned in, and kissed me on the cheek. She didn't answer right away, remaining suspended at eye level, while she searched my face with her piercing blue eyes.

"I would love to come over for dinner."

Being in such a close proximity to Molly, made me weak at the knees. I was tempted to pull her onto my lap and to just keep showering her with more and more kisses.

But then I realized it was 3:30 in the afternoon and she probably had more clients to see.

I settled for brushing her hair behind her ear and returning her kiss with one of my own.

Molly straightened up to her 5' 6" height and glanced toward the clock on the wall, "I should probably get back to work."

"Of course." I remembered the other thing I was going to ask her and stopped short at the door, "Do you like steak?"

"I like the occasional steak. That would be a nice treat. I should be done here around 6:30. Will that be alright?"

"Perfect. See you soon."

I was still floating on air long after I got home.

I had gone overboard on my purchase of candles, but who cared?

All ten of them were lined up, two by two, down the center of the dining room table. It was set with the nice China, and silverware that I'd polished until it gleamed and glistened.

When all the prep work was done, I set about planning for the following day, I needed to get up super early to head toward Nashville. I couldn't justify splurging on a hotel room right now.

I would drive up early and straight back. Then maybe I would see if Molly would like to take advantage of my last day of freedom to watch a romantic movie.

What would I wear for this momentous occasion?

I decided Molly should see me for once, in clothes that weren't completely battered to all hell and back, or falling off of me.

I chose a pair of dark jeans and a black Lacoste shirt that used to be a little tight, but now fit like a glove. I shaved off the stubble that had been accumulating for a few days and took a pair of scissors to my hair so that it wasn't so shaggy looking. I even put on aftershave.

The end result was not half bad. Without the dark circles, I no longer looked like a heroin addict. One might even say that I looked kind of handsome.

At 6:30 on the dot, Molly knocked on the screen door.

I let her in, leaning down to kiss her on cheek for the second time today. I didn't think I would ever get tired of doing so. "What's this?"

"I made a chocolate cake between clients," she said and handed it to me, but I could see that she was taking in my sudden transformation with a hard to read expression on her face.

She certainly looked beautiful, in jeans as well, and wearing a pink eyelet shirt that was tied in the back with a kind of boho-hippy vibe.

She wore her hair down, very little makeup, and pair of crocheted earrings that looked like roses.

"You look gorgeous." I found it infinitely endearing that she blushed.

"So do you. You look younger this way."

I felt younger, unburdened the way I'd been in my early twenties. I felt full of endless possibilities.

And even though I still had the weight of my mother's illness, which was by no means, a walk in the park, I was prepared to tackle it, head on, and embrace it with radical acceptance.

"Thanks!" I carried the cake into the dining room. "Would you like a glass of wine?"

"That would be nice."

I heard her gasp as she laid eyes upon the many candles that were the only source of light in the room. I'd purchased a bouquet of daisies that I had cut off at the top of the stem and scattered along the table.

"Hal, this is so lovely." Her hand rose to her mouth and I could see in the dark that she was really taken aback.

"Are you crying?"

She nodded and I gently wrapped my arm around her shoulders. "I wanted to make you happy, not to upset you."

"No. I'm not upset," she wiped away tears and grinned. "It's just so touching. It's so, so sweet, like the sweetness in the center of a pie, that kind of goodness, that you did this for me."

"Molly Owens! This is not nearly as much as you deserve. Not even close."

Her reaction made me feel that I might not be worthy of her, like she was a thing of starlight, an otherworldly presence that I might never truly comprehend.

It made me want to be better, to do more, just so that I could earn the right to exist alongside her.

"Hal, I have to tell you something. It's something I should have told you already, but it never seemed like the appropriate time."

"Ok. But first, you sit here, and I'll get us some wine."

When I returned, I noticed she had placed one of the daisies behind her ear. She took the glass and a big swig before saying, "Your father has been haunting me."

I swallowed hard, in a weird way that went down wrong and I caused me to cough. Once recovered, I said, "I don't even know who my father is, Molly. How could that be?"

"Well, it started right before your mother went into the hospital, before you came here and brought Rita home. He came to me in the middle of the night and woke me from a dream. He showed me images that I've been trying to piece together. It's funny because, all spirits are different, the way they can communicate, the things they choose to show me. He kept showing me a cup of coffee, that's how I knew his name. A cup of Joe. His name was Joe. And then he showed me images of a young Rita with him. And then he showed me that he had died very young."

She paused long enough to allow this to sink in.

I thought back to the first time I had seen her, on the street in front of the house, talking to someone named, Joe, "I saw you one day while you were walking. You were arguing with someone. You told someone to leave you alone."

"That was your father. See, he tried to get me to talk to Rita, but she was not right, Hal. I could see that she had some sort of dementia. That's why I kept an eye on her. I was afraid for her well-being."

"According to my mother, my father was a no-good criminal, a dead beat," I said.

"I don't think that's the whole story. Joe has shown me a card, the 10 of diamonds in the upright. For me, that represents great generational wealth and abundance. I think he must have died before you were even born."

"Did you get a last name for him?" I asked.

"No, but he kept pointing to the red diamond. It was more like he was showing that it was also a symbol for something else. But he couldn't get me to understand."

"Hold that thought." I rushed to the living room to retrieve my laptop, pulled up the website for Chandley & Stewart, and pointed to their logo, "Is this what he showed you?"

"That's it. What does it mean, though?"

"I think it means, that my father is somehow linked to a trust, set up by one of the founders of this law firm. It was the thing I was going to get your help with the other night. There is a mysterious trust that was set up for my mother by a man named William Chandley, but I don't think this man was my father. And they won't give me any information over the phone."

Molly sighed, "I wish I knew what the connection was. It's not always so clear what spirit is trying to tell me. I've ruined this nice romantic evening, haven't I?"

I took her hand in mine and squeezed it, "Not at all. Your timing couldn't be any more perfect. I have an appointment to meet with someone at that firm tomorrow, in Nashville. I'd like for you to come with me."

Molly perked up, "Really?"

"Really. Can you do that?"

"I don't have any appointments scheduled, so yes. I would like to come."

"Now, can we start over? Molly Owens, how do you like your steak cooked."

She laughed and nervously twirled a piece of her hair around her finger, "Just run it through the fire a little."

I got the coals started and cleaned up the grill while Molly finished up the salad and pulled the baked potatoes out of the oven.

We settled down to eat and all else was forgotten. She told me about growing up, the youngest of three sisters, and about how her entire family had uncanny intuition that had always made it hard for them to fit in.

I understood this feeling of never fitting in, but for different reasons. For me it had been taking on the shame of my circumstances, the darkness that robbed me of stability and love.

But in Molly's family there had been lots of love. They clung to each other because they really got each other, and the weirdness that others did not.

"Your family sounds like a lot of fun. I think my life might have been easier if I had had siblings,"

"Or it might have made it harder for you to walk away. You would have been pulled back by the toxicity. And you would not be where you are now."

I nodded. "I've forgiven myself for that. For walking out on her all those years ago."

"Then you are in a prime position, Hal Winston. Most people never get this far."

I turned the subject back to Molly. I wanted to know everything about her.

"Did you grow up in Tennessee?" I asked.

"Nope. Mobile, Alabama. My father got a deal on a property near the beach. Not a house. He bought a little old white church by a cemetery and turned it into our home."

"You lived in a church?"

"I did. And let me tell you that it was a magical place. See nobody wanted to buy it because it was known to be haunted. You never know with these things. I mean, they could really be dark places, you know. But when he got there, he said he could feel this angelic energy all around the place. That was all he needed to know."

"Your dad sounds like an interesting person. Is he still living?"

Molly finished chewing a bite of her salad, "Yes. He's a heart surgeon. A very good one I might add." When she saw my expression she said, "I think you would be surprised at just how many people in the medical field are extremely, intuitive. Often this guides them in their work with patients. They just don't talk about it."

I thought about Nancy and her just having the feeling that something wasn't right with mother that day she was so sick.

"And your mother?" I asked.

"Her work is volunteering in the community. Running charities, raising money for homeless shelters, library funds, and whatever cause needs championing. I've been fortunate to have the upbringing I did. I never fail to be grateful for it and what my family taught me about caring for other people."

"Did you have any visitors from the cemetery? And by visitors, I do mean, ghosts."

She finished chewing a bite of steak, "Uh-huh, all the time. It was an old historical one, so lots of woman in dresses that looked like torture devices and civil war soldiers. They would pass through the house sometimes."

"This never scared you?"

"Not really. I think that's because my family were level headed about these things. They didn't have any fear about it, so neither did I. What was weird was being around people who couldn't see or sense these things. And for a long time, feeling like I had to wear a mask to make people feel comfortable."

"You know, growing up, people on this street always said the house you are living in now was haunted."

"Not with spirits. But it had sort of a melancholy energy, probably because it was a rental property and lots of people had left their energy behind there. When the realtor told me how much they wanted for it, way below its value, I told her I wanted to see it. I asked her if she could wait for me outside, and I walked through and did a clearing of the whole house, and surrounding property. Then I walked back through again and saw its charm, all the things that would make it perfect for me. And I bought it. And have never regretted that decision."

"I have something to confess. There used to be a treehouse behind your house, and when my mother was in one of her rages, there was many a night, I slept in it. I was happy when there wasn't a tenant living in your house, because I felt safe there, like I was connected to that house."

Her face grew sad, maybe at the thought of me being so alone, "That may say more about you than you realize, Hal Winston."

"How did you even end up in Piney View?"

"After I graduated from UT, I got a position with the department of human resources, working in this area. It was tough for me, seeing really hard things, feeling so much, and not being able to change anything. After five years, spirit said, *enough! Time to get with the program. You can't heal people if you aren't being your authentic self.*"

"Do you ever feel burdened by it? Ever want to live a normal kind of life?"

"I'm not normal. I wasn't put here to have a normal life." She placed her silverware down and glanced down at her empty plate. "Thank you, for inviting me over to share this lovely meal with you."

"You're welcome, Molly. Thank you for agreeing to go with me tomorrow. It will be nice to have someone in my corner for a change."

We cleared our dinner plates to the kitchen sink.

Molly cut a couple of small pieces of the cake she had baked. It was hands down the best chocolate cake I'd ever eaten. Perhaps, it was because she had infused it with pure love.

Afterwards, we sat in comfortable silence, finishing the last of our wine in the glow of candlelight that danced about the room.

The opened window invited the outside world to rush in toward us. Nearby, a whippoorwill cried out soulfully.

Had Molly noticed it?

I couldn't help but to think it was meant for me, a harbinger of something unpleasant and inevitable that waited ahead.

CHAPTER TWENTY-THREE

It was 7:30 am when we parked inside the garage for the office building that housed Chandley & Stewart.

The building was extremely modern, a slate grey façade mostly composed of rectangular glass windows that reached from floor to ceiling on each of its five levels.

The offices, located on the third floor, wouldn't open for another thirty minutes, but Molly felt staff would be in the office already, and she was right.

Tracy came out from the back. She was a pretty, fiftyish woman, who looked polished and crisp in her dark pantsuit and red silk shirt.

She led us to a private room where everything looked expensive. The Persian rug probably cost more than my Bronco. There, coffee, Danish pastries, and an assortment of muffins were waiting.

"Help yourself. I'll come and get you as soon as they are ready for you," she said.

I wasn't sure why I felt so nervous. Molly put her hand on my knee to stop it from erratically bobbing up and down.

"Sorry," I said.

"Whatever you learn today, try to look at it from a higher perspective. You can be bitter, or you can be better, but you can never be both," she said.

"Right. Better not bitter. Better not bitter, "I said this several times, like the words were a mantra that would make them become a reality.

I just had this knowing, that what I learned today would alter the understanding I had about my life, that it would turn my perceptions upside down.

And I knew Molly felt this way too. I could see it in her eyes. She was worried that it would hurt me somehow.

I whispered even though we were alone in the waiting room, "Is Joe here with you?"

She shook her head, "No, the past month, he hasn't been around at all."

"Probably off with little Hal, stirring up trouble someplace else. It's funny how they both disappeared just as things started to get interesting."

Molly chuckled at this, "That does seem to be the case."

"It's really very, very, very annoying. If you see either of those yahoos, please let them know I'm not too happy about being left in the dark to sort through cryptic messages from the beyond."

This only made her chuckle more. "Are you sure you want me to tell them that? Spirit does have a sense of humor. It might only get you a lot more of the same."

"Then tell little Hal he's grounded the minute he's born. And I will not be swayed by little baby coos or the sweet smell. No, I will not."

Molly clamped her lips together to stop the smile that threatened, "Will do. Should I ever see him again, I will give him that stern warning."

Our playful banter was cut short when Tracy returned, "They are ready for you now."

I wondered who "they" were. It somehow made this feel a lot more serious. Did it really require a team of experts to answer my questions regarding the trust?

Shit, maybe I should have brought my own lawyer. I just had no idea what I was walking into. I was glad to have Molly by my side.

Tracy opened the door to a meeting room that held a massive, round, mahogany table and plush leather chairs. Three men stood up as we entered and I glanced over at Molly before we took our seats.

Ambush, I thought.

Molly smiled as if she'd heard this thought, as if to say, *we've got this.*

The confident looking one, who looked too young to have already finished law school, extended his hand.

This expensive suit wearing, pubescent adolescent was the leader? The world was run by children now.

"Hello, Mr. Winston. I'm Mark Howard," he said. And then he made things really awkward by asking, "Is this Mrs. Winston?"

A borderline cherry red rose into Molly's cheeks, "No, I'm Molly Owens."

Mr. Howard waited a few seconds as if he expected an explanation of her relationship to me to follow.

But Molly made no effort to explain why she was here, staring back unflinchingly, her quiet and polite way of letting him know that it was none of his business.

He cleared his throat after his failed attempt to solicit more information, "Please, have a seat."

He motioned to the man on his right, "This is Thomas Spencer, an associate here at the firm." Then he motioned toward the elderly man sitting to his left, "And this is Martin Chandley, the brother of William Chandley, the man who set up the trust for your mother."

After the introductions, he said, "Let's get started."

We waited for him to sift through a stack of papers before pulling one of them out. He pointed to a clause at the bottom, "Here we can see where William wrote a statement in his own words explaining why he established this trust. He read them out loud.

These funds shall be held in trust and distributed monthly to Rita Winston in the amount of $800 per month. Upon her death the entirety of the remaining funds shall be released to her son, Halbert Thomas Winston, in honor of his own son, Joseph Edelton Chandley.

"Joseph, he was my father, wasn't he?"

Martin Chandley leaned forward. He had only a few wispy strands of silver hair left on his head. The hand that tremored slightly, fell onto the table, revealing skin as thin as the paper we were all staring at.

Martin had to be in his eighties.

"William was my older brother. He was fifteen years my senior and we were never what you could call close. He was a rigid man. When your father fell in love with Rita, William did not approve of this match. He felt that they were unevenly yoked. He told your father that if he married Rita, he would disown him for good."

"So, my father kicked my mother to the curb."

The man looked pained by this, "Yes. But not because of the money. Your father had been diagnosed with non-Hodgkin's lymphoma around the same time. He knew that he needed his father's money to be able to afford the best treatments to fight it. Your father cut things off with Rita but she was not having it. She went to my brother and informed him that she was pregnant. William tried to pay her to end it, but she refused. He never told her about your father's illness, and he never told Joseph that she was pregnant. He lied. He told Joseph that your mother had accepted money to go away."

"What kind of person would do something like that?" It was so incredibly cruel that it had spun me into an incredulous anger.

Martin sighed, "Not a very good one. But he did grow to regret this. I'm sure, had your father lived, that he would have found Rita and learned the truth. But that was not to be."

He paused to take a handkerchief out of his pocket and wiped his eyes. It appeared that he had captured these tears the instant they had formed. "William grieved after Joseph died. He began to believe that he had really died because his heart had been broken. The trust was born from his guilt around this. You were a secret in the family, only a few of us knew anything about you."

"And I wasn't worthy enough to belong in it, I guess."

"Your mother was angry. After she received word of Joseph's death. She threatened to go to every Nashville paper there was to expose our underhanded ways if any of us came within ten feet of either of you. She never wanted the money, so William set up an account on her behalf, and the statements were mailed to her from the law firm every month."

"It sounds like her reaction was pretty convenient for you all. That way you could all say you tried, when deep down you know you didn't," I was disgusted with it all and didn't want to believe that I shared the same bloodline with such a cold and calculating lot of people.

It left a bitter taste in my mouth and I thought about what Molly had said earlier, better not bitter.

Better not bitter. Breathe, Hal.

"I can't deny that was true in the beginning. But as William aged, he tried harder, writing letters that Rita sent back to him, unopened. It had been too long. He was ashamed to come to you. Ashamed of the ultimatum that had robbed Joseph of the little time he could have spent with you and your mother. The rest of William's life, this ate away at him. When he died, he left a large portion of his estate to her. Rita could have claimed it at any time but she hasn't touched any of it."

I thought about how this rejection of my mother had shaped her, contributing to her bitterness and anger at the world. She had never been able to escape it, not until the dementia came along and forced her to.

And through this forgetting, somehow forgiveness between us had been forged.

"I'm sorry, but I can't muster any sympathy for William Chandley at the moment. It might take some time for me to get to that place, if I ever do." I wasn't sure how I felt, exactly.

Was I furious? Sad? Or relieved to know my father's name? And to learn that he hadn't been a horrible person?

Molly reached for my hand underneath the table and squeezed it tightly. This simple gesture, calmed me.

"I would love for you to meet the family, for us to build a bridge of a sort, and get know each other. I know it's a tad late, but we are willing to give it a try, should you decide to forgive us," Martin said.

"I'm not sure if I will ever want to be connected to any of you. I feel for my mother, and for Joseph. It's all so heartbreaking and it did so much damage that it's hard to even quantify."

The other attorney chose this time to enter the conversation and I realized that this man, likely represented the interests of the Chandley family. "Mr. Winston, we hope we will not have to quarrel over any inheritance. We feel that the amount left by William was a fair share of your father's portion of the estate."

He had taken my words completely out of context, jumping in to demonstrate his willingness to act as the shark of an attorney that he was, to do battle with me should he have to.

"Whoa! Hey. I'm not talking about money. What is wrong with you people?"

He pointed his gold embossed pen in my direction and began anew, in almost the same tone-deaf manner, "I only wanted to clarify the fact that you have received a fair share of—"

"STOP! Not another word from you or I'll find a place that is not too pleasant to shove that pen."

The unified team of strangers regarded me with concern. Perhaps they had heard stories about how my mother was prone to unhinged fits of rage and was a danger to the world.

But the reality was, these people didn't know what to do when the meagerest hint of emotion came into play. When faced with it, they became spineless, cold-blooded jellyfish.

Whatever they had been planning to say was interrupted when my phone rang in my pocket. I recognized Nancy's ringtone.

"I have to take this. Excuse me."

I walked out into the hallway leaving Molly seated at the table. I thought it might even do them some good to be exposed to her energy for a little bit. "Hey, Nancy."

"I just got a call from the facility. Your mother had a stroke less than an hour ago. I'm so sorry, Hal. She's been unresponsive."

"Shit! I'm in Nashville. Can you let them know that I'm leaving here now and will be there at soon as I can?"

"Absolutely. Don't be reckless. Drive carefully, okay."

I promised that I would and stuck my head into the conference room, "I need to cut this short. My mother has had a stroke."

Molly gathered her purse, met me at the door, and took my hand inside her own. I cast a dismissive nod toward the others.

But Thomas Chaplin, hopped out of his seat and jogged toward us, "Wait, Mr. Winston. Your packet. All the information you requested is in here. And some other documents we felt you should have."

I took the thick envelope without looking at him. None of this stuff mattered at the moment. What mattered was that my mother had taken a turn for the worse. And I needed to get there as soon as possible.

I tossed the keys to Molly, "It might be better if you drive."

She started the engine, adjusted the mirrors, and said, "You did well in there. I'm proud of you."

I leaned in then and kissed her on the mouth, letting the sweetness of it soak into me and pull me back momentarily from being totally devastated.

Molly pulled away, brushed my cheek with her lips, and slid the car into reverse. A silence fell over us and I was glad for it. It allowed me to put my thoughts in order.

My father hadn't really abandoned me.

My mother had shielded me from his family.

But why?

Was it because she wanted to protect me from being hurt by them, the same way that she had been?

Maybe her love for me all these years had been expressed in the form of protection. She had weaponized her anger and turned it into a shield.

Then she had sought to harden me, so that this kind of betrayal could never touch me.

I opened the butterfly clasp on the manila envelope and sorted through it. There was bank information, routing number and account number. There was a copy of documents for the trust, and also, a copy of William Chandley's will.

At the bottom, a bulk of smaller envelopes had settled. They were letters, addressed to my mother from William Chandley.

All of them had been sent back with, *return to sender,* written in my mother's sloppy handwriting. The last date was October 8, 1995.

On this one, she had written, *stop these immediately, or I will take action.* I drew in a deep breath and opened it.

Dear Rita,

My time on this earth will not be long now. My doctors have advised me to get my affairs in order, as I may not last until the end of this month.
There is not a day that goes by that I do not think about Joseph and how I wronged him, and how I wronged you and

Halbert. There is no greater crime than standing against love, stopping it, crushing it. I do not understand the evil thing inside of me that felt justified in doing so. I am ashamed.

All those years ago, I told you that you would never be accepted in the circles of society that we operated within. I revealed who I truly was and you saw and understood, perfectly that I was the snake in the garden of Eden. You need to know that Joseph never stopped loving you. And he died broken hearted because of a lie.

I told him that I offered you money to go away and that you accepted it. I never told him that you were pregnant.

I know that I do not deserve your forgiveness, although I hope that you someday will find it within yourself to do so. And upon your death, when my grandson reads these letters and learns of what I have done, I hope that he will forgive me for this treachery and know that his father was a kind and loving man. He deserved so much more than what he received in this life.

Rita, I have been informed that you sometimes visit Joseph's grave, directly across from where your mother and grandparents are buried. I have also purchased the plot next to him for you, should you decide to use it when the time comes.

I was wrong about you, Rita. You are an honorable woman. I am sorry for hurting you.

Much Regret,

William Chandley

It hit me suddenly, the memory of going to the graves of my grandparents and leaving flowers for them. There were times when my mother brought an extra bouquet, and left it on one of the graves.

When I was maybe nine or ten, old enough to notice that the name on the grave was different from our own, I'd asked her, "Who is this person and why do you care about him?"

"He was important to me once," she had said, with a softness to her eyes that was uncharacteristic. But quickly, it had been gone, "Mind your business. Don't worry about what I do."

And that was one hundred percent what I had done, never giving it another thought. Until now.

I turned to Molly, "He's buried in Piney View."

I could tell that I'd pulled Molly out of her own deep thoughts, "Who is?"

"My father. William had him buried there to be close to my mother. She used to leave flowers for him." I filled her in on the details of the letter.

"It's so tragic. I'm very sorry, Hal. How are you feeling about all of this?"

"I might be in shock. I don't know. I feel numb, but also like I've been robbed. Like somebody broke into my house and took something really valuable that I never knew that I had before it was gone."

"Why do you think Rita never opened those letters?" Molly asked as she took the exit for I-40.

"I don't know. She knew about the grave. She put flowers on that grave all these years. And she let me believe that my father was a horrible man whom I was better off not knowing anything about."

Molly turned to me as if she'd had a sudden epiphany, "I think I may understand. She might have sensed that if she knew all the details, the extent of what had actually been taken from her, that she wouldn't have been able to bear it with her fragile mental health."

I thought back to what Molly had said about the future already existing and how some of us were aware of this on some level, "You think my mother knew it would break her heart? And because of this, she spent her life running from this truth, rather than facing it?"

"I do."

"Everything feels like a dream. Mamma's illness. Even you. Like I've skipped a time loop or something, like it's unfolding the way it was always meant to, at the exact time it was always designed to. And as hard as it is and has been, it still feels like a—"

"Like a gift?"

I stared at Molly's profile, the curves of her high cheek bones, the impossible length of her lashes. "Yes. Why do I feel like this?"

Molly checked her rearview mirror, slowed down, and set the cruise control, "Because you've leveled up, Hal. You were supposed to learn certain things, to make certain choices, things that were really hard. And you did. You made the right choices. Everything is in synch and feels serendipitous because you are heading in the right direction."

I looked at her with my mouth wide open. How could she be this, infused with all this love in a way that it spilled out into everything and everyone she touched.

It made me feel safe, like whatever happened, it would be okay. I would okay. The world would be okay.

We arrived at Sunset Acute Care Center. Molly pulled up to the front door and said, "I'll let you out. I'm not sure what to do. Do you want me to come inside? Or if you would like time alone, I could always come back later."

"For Pete's sake, Molly. Without you, I think I would just feel like somebody licked the red right off of my candy."

I mostly wanted to lighten the mood before we faced whatever we were going to find in there. But also, I wanted her to know how deeply my feelings for her really ran.

Molly grinned, "Smartass. You go ahead. I'll park the car and then I'll come find you."

I got out, "At least you don't think I'm a dumbass. Cause that would hurt my feelings."

Molly just rolled her eyes and shooed me out of the car. I watched her drive away and prolonged the inevitable, waiting several seconds more before entering the building.

I found the front desk. A man with a thin covering of light brown hair and double chin that didn't match the rest of his relatively fit body, glanced up from his cup of coffee, "How can I help you?"

"I'm Hal Winston. My mother is Rita Winston."

"Hello, Mr. Winston. I'm Jake. She's in room 101. Rita had been in a good mood, telling us all kinds of stories. Then all of sudden she starting getting agitated, and the stroke followed."

"Has she started responding at all?"

"Not really. She was struggling with her breathing, so we started giving her a small amount of morphine to help relax her. She is resting comfortably at the moment."

I thanked Jake and found Mamma's room. Only the foot of the hospital bed was visible when I pushed open the door. I knew it was my mother because the light blue crocheted blanket that I'd sent with her, was folded across at her feet.

It was shocking to fully view her. Her head was turned toward her left side. Her mouth was open, cheeks sunken in. In just a few days, she had changed. There was a grey spectrum to her skin and she didn't even look like the woman I'd said goodbye to a few days ago.

I moved closer, clasped her left hand that was strangely stiff, drawn into an awkward open-fistedness, and listened. The wet crackling sound coming from her chest with each breath, was concerning.

There was a name for it. They called it, the death rattle.

"Mamma, it's Hal." I waited for a response, for her eyes to open, or for her to suddenly jump to attention and start ordering me about.

But she didn't stir.

There were things I wanted to say before it was too late. I needed to speak these truths aloud, to clear out the foul, deceptive air that had surrounded us for so long.

"Mamma, I don't know what will happen now. I'm here for you, no matter what. Please know that you are safe. I need to tell you something that may be hard to hear. I know about my father, Joseph. He wasn't a bad man. His father lied to him. All those letters William Chandley wrote to you, were pleas for your forgiveness, a confession of what he had done. Until the day he died, he felt shame over keeping the two of you apart. Joseph never stopped loving you."

I thought I felt the slightest movement of her pinky finger. I squeezed her hand, waited, but there was no other indication that she had understood me.

"I don't want this to upset you. I'm saying these things so that you will know that you were loved. That you are loved. I love you, Mamma. And I know that you love me. I want you to know that I know that."

Our faces were only inches apart. I stroked her hair back over her pillow and noticed a muscle twitch at her temple.

And then I saw it. A tear rolled from the corner of her left eye and trickled down her cheek. I leaned in and planted a butterfly kiss upon her eyelid.

Then I wiped her tear away, and said, "Enough with this sappy stuff. How about we listen to some Elvis."

I selected a Christmas album.

Some might think that was a ridiculous musical selection for that moment. I mean most people would have probably chosen one with his gospel songs. And it wasn't even close to Christmas.

Why a Christmas album?

But there were only two things I knew, without a shadow of a doubt, that actually made my mother happy. Christmas and Elvis. So why not give her both?

Molly found us and tiptoed into the room. She listened for only a second and said, "Oh. I love this song." And began to sing along, her voice lovely and perfect.

Lord, help me. How I loved this strange and wonderful woman.

CHAPTER TWENTY-FOUR

Do you remember how I said that you never knew that you were in a particular kind of moment until you were on the other side of it?

Like, I didn't know that Mamma would never flip me off again, or call out my name in a way that implied she'd fallen haphazardly into a pit full of venomous snakes.

I didn't know that I wouldn't go through yet another night of sundowning or cook her an experimental meal that would either get the puss face or over the top praise for its deliciousness.

I didn't know when I said goodbye before she came to this facility that she would never return home.

These moments, the good and the bad, ran together seamlessly.

In the good moments, were we ever really present enough to appreciate them?

During the bad, did we ever think that we would get through them?

But the thing about these moments was, that if we had presence of mind to truly be grounded in them, to allow ourselves to experience the weight and fullness of them, if we weren't avoidant, we would have fewer regrets.

When time did run out, we'd already have our longer goodbye, expressed in the whole of that relationship.

Only, nobody lived in a perfect world. Most of us, ended up with some kind of regret; We had regrets for what was said or wasn't said, done or not done, for how we failed to support another person, and all the ways that we fell short.

But we shouldn't.

Molly said that when people reach out to her from the other side with messages to loved ones, it is almost always with the desire to relieve that person of the burden of guilt and regret.

You see, we've already been forgiven. We just need to forgive ourselves.

We need to hug ourselves and to tell ourselves that we did the best that the people we were in that moment could have done. Then we should say a little prayer in the wind and let it all go.

Sometimes, this was the only closure that we'd ever get. And that was okay.

Molly and I held vigil in room 101 overnight and into the following day. The nurses were extremely kind and accommodating, bringing us coffee and trays of food from the cafeteria.

We slept in chairs and held Mamma's hands. We sang to her. We rubbed lotion on her arms. We brushed her hair. Whatever we could do really, to comfort her. But her final moment rushed in swiftly.

Molly was the first to notice that something had changed. She threw off her blanket and rose from the chair she'd been dozing in.

From the thin fog of sleep, I heard all of this, but didn't open my eyes until she whispered, "Hal. Wake up."

I bolted up and pressed my ear closer to Mamma's chest, listening to her labored breathing.

Then she began to cough and sputter.

"I'll get the nurse," Molly said.

The evening nurse, Roxanne, rushed in with a syringe of morphine that she dropped into Mamma's mouth. In just a couple of minutes, her coughing and distressed breathing, eased.

She looked peaceful again.

Molly got up and poured herself a cup of coffee from a thermos the staff had left for us. She pulled her chair close enough to place her free hand lovingly on my mother's arm.

I felt anxious.

Was it because I knew that Molly sensed things that I could not? Or was it because I knew too, that we had shifted into a new phase?

In the sink, I washed away crusty eyes and pulled my chair directly opposite Molly, on the other side of the bed. I squeezed my mother's hand.

I smiled at Molly's tousled hair, full of rat's nests, and her mascara smeared eyes.

It was so utterly endearing, this complete unawareness of herself, and so adorable, that I wanted to pick her up and hug her, the way one hugged tiny, precious things, like baby animals.

I felt Mamma's hand move for the first time since we'd arrived.

I tried to make it happen again. A gently squeeze. Pause. Gentle squeeze. Pause. On the third try, I felt the muscles in her hand contract.

She had responded. I was sure. And I knew that it had taken a lot for her to coordinate this simple gesture.

"We're here for you. There is nothing to be afraid of. If you need to go, if this is too much, you can let go now, Mamma. I'll be alright. Joseph and little Hal will be waiting there for you."

Tears blinded me. But I tried to keep this from coming across in my voice. I lifted the edge of the sheet from the bed and wiped them away.

Molly sat silently, watching us, her smile equal parts of melancholy and joy. Tears fell from her own eyes but she seemed not to notice them.

Mamma gasped for breath.

I moved quickly to sit her up, hoping this would help her breathe better. With my hand pressed against her back, I could feel the struggle within her, her heart working so hard.

There was another sharp gasp. A gentle exhale. And her heart stopped beating.

She was gone.

The other thing we never knew when we were in these moments, was which one would be our last.

And when it finally came, those of us left behind, were shocked. Because even though we had known that it was inevitable, we never really thought the time would ever come.

We expected another rally call, or the force of that person's will to drag them back, yet again, from the abyss.

I wrapped Rita Winston up in my arms and wept until my eyes stung and my chest hurt, until I'd released everything that needed to be.

At some point, I felt Molly's arms around me. Then the staff came in and took my mother away.

The rest was a blur.

I don't know who gathered up Mamma's things and placed them in a large shopping bag. Maybe, Molly did.

I don't remember the drive back home, or what time it had been.

Later, I had to get all of these details from Molly.

Rita Winston died at 9:55 pm. on a Thursday.

Arrangements were made to have her interred next to my father.

This was not an easy decision to make given my mother's past feelings. And Molly had not gotten any guidance from the other side, either.

Old Rita would have threatened all sorts of terrible, haunting scenarios. But the new, Alzheimer's Rita, would have been happy to forgive the past. That Rita would have felt gratitude.

I tried to be at ease with this decision. I was for the most part.

And then one day I discovered a copy of my mother's will. It was in the weirdest place possible, taped against the back of her closet, behind her winter coats.

It was dated to a time when I was still a student at UT, the same period when she had created the other document giving me the power to make decisions on her behalf.

She left everything to me. And her wish was to be buried at Hallway Cemetery in a previously purchased lot, next to Joseph Chandley.

She did not however, leave a letter behind to explain any of this to me. I suppose she knew I would figure it all out once I discovered the trust.

And as for the trust account and inheritance. Well, that was a silver lining to everything.

My mother had never touched a dime of it. I suppose to her, it was blood money, and to touch it meant to give William Chandley what she didn't want to give him, atonement.

I believed her desire for me to have it all, was her way of saying, I'm sorry, and making up for everything that had gone wrong between us.

I believed whatever bad had been attached to this money, had been laundered clean, through the healing that had taken place. All I needed to do now was to use it in a way that would honor the memory of everyone attached to it.

It was a sizable amount of moolah. I'm not going to lie. It would be enough to pay for me going back to school to get my master's degree, then my PhD, and to still be sitting pretty.

As far as making connections with distant family. I wasn't there, not yet. But the flowers the Chandley family sent for the service were pretty spectacular, lining the entire aisle between my mother and father's graves.

The service was a simple graveside affair, on a Monday afternoon. I asked Pastor Bob to do the honors.

Only a few people showed up, some neighbors, Nancy and Janine came together, a woman named Ellie, whom had worked with my mother at the diner for twenty years, and of course, Molly Owens.

If I had to describe that day, I would say it was full of incoming fall winds, that it was saturated with the earthy decay of leaves, still wet from a morning rain shower, the sun peeking out from behind the clouds, and the promise and potential of all the good things lurking just around the corner.

It felt as though the spell, that had caused a reign of darkness to fall over our family, had been broken.

Pastor Bob kept his sermon short. But it was powerful. He hadn't known my mother long, but his short visits had given him glimpses into the many dimensions of her, good and bad.

He had no trouble extracting what had been noble about her, or the nuances that made her the way she was. He had us laughing about the tale of the egg on the preacher's chair that would never have a proper ending.

Through this, I twirled the ring in my pocket around my finger. It was an engagement ring that had belonged to my great grandmother.

I'm not sure why I brought it. If it was because it made me feel as though I was bringing this ancestor along with us? Or if I'd really brought it, hoping to work up the nerve to ask Molly Owens to marry me?

If I'd ever been certain about anything in this world, it was her. And I didn't want to waste any more of my days in it.

That evening, Molly and I set about transforming the neighborhood with luminaries, white paper bags that we had filled with sand and white votive candles. They cast their warm glow up and down Gilbert Street.

A giant outdoor projector was erected in my mother's front yard. A long banquet table was draped with a nice tablecloth. Plates and silverware, platters of fried chicken, corn on the cob, and fried cherry pies were set out.

It was while we finished setting up the round tables and chairs we'd rented for guests, that I asked Molly what it was that had alerted her that things had shifted on the night my mother died.

"I could hear a high frequency all around us and then the room filled with spirits, her parents, grandparents, your father. And there were higher beings there too, angelic ones, so many of them, woven around her like a fine tapestry of white light. It was beautiful. I wanted to tell you then what I saw. But I knew it would have only overwhelmed you, and I didn't want it to take away from your last minutes with Rita."

"You were right to do that. It would have. I was stunned at how fast it all happened."

"It's because you gave her permission, when you told her that you would be alright. It released her."

"Is that really how it works? That we hang on to this world sometimes just because of obligation to others?"

It seemed an odd concept to me that all my mother had needed to pass on, was my consent.

"Think of it like going on a trip, making sure all the doors are locked and that the coffee pot has been turned off, so that they can enjoy that trip without worrying about what they are leaving behind. They stay for us, Hal. And you weren't selfish, you didn't try to keep her here so that you could resolve deep seated issues between the two of you. You let her go. Because you are strong. And you know the only person who can do that for you, is you."

"I wish I'd tried to repair my relationship with my mother a long time ago."

"Don't you go doing that. What ifs are only good for wallpapering the doghouse, if that. There is such a thing as divine timing, whether you believe in it or not. You reach a level of understanding, and that opens a doorway to another level, then another. And the events that unfold all around you on each of those levels, those are your lessons. Only God decides when you've learned them. But we get lots of chances because he has shitloads of patience."

"I feel like I need to turn that into a T-shirt, *God has shitloads of patience.*"

I wasn't completely joking. That would make a great slogan.

She went on to say that, if you suddenly find that you are going against the grain, against the wind, against a swarm of locusts, that just means you need to change your thinking and see the higher perspective, because there is something that you are missing. Somehow, you've taken a wrong turn.

Before I could change my mind or talk myself out of it, I reached into my pocket and pulled out the ring. Molly was unfolding a metal chair and hadn't noticed that I had kneeled down next to her.

In fact, she almost tripped over me. Then came the confusion, the lifting of her eyebrows, the recognition of what this gesture meant, and a hand flew to her mouth.

"Molly Owens, I love you. I know we haven't known each other long, but I don't care. I know what you are to me. I want to bring that pain in the butt, little Hal, into being someday. And I want to do that with you. Will you marry me?"

Molly smiled sweetly through her tears. Then she rolled her eyes, "Well, duh. Of course, I will. Little Hal already told me that I was going to be his mother someday."

I slipped the ring on her finger and was amazed that it fit her perfectly. Then I stood up and wiped away her tears.

"You told me he didn't give you that information."

She shrugged, "I didn't want to influence your feelings for me. And that definitely, would have. I didn't want to spend my life wondering if you had only become interested in me because of that."

"Makes sense. But now I have to wonder if little Hal influenced your feelings about me."

She became serious then. It was impossible to doubt the truth when I looked into the depths of her sapphire eyes. They sparkled like jewels in the orange hue of the setting sun, "I knew the day I watched you set that mattress on fire, that you were the one."

Molly held up her hand to look at the ring I'd placed there. "This is lovely. Very simple and elegant like the woman who wore it before me. It belonged to your great grandmother, didn't it?"

"It did."

I don't know why I was surprised that she had gleaned that from touching the ring, but I was. And I wondered if one day it would all feel normal, this being connected to someone who could see so many things that I could not. I kind of felt like it would.

We'd invited everyone who lived on the street to a celebration of my mother's life, and also, the staff we'd worked with at hospice. Pastor Bob brought his beautiful wife, Maybelle, along.

It wasn't a sad affair, more like a fancy block party than anything. There was a lot of laughter and excitement about the engagement.

After dinner we broke open the champagne, pouring them into clear plastic flutes.

I gave the first toast, "Mamma, could spin some yarns. She had this memory of us sending off Chinese lanterns. This never happened. We never did this. But it was such a beautiful memory, nonetheless. One of the last things she asked before she died was if we could do the lanterns again."

A sudden gush of emotion threatened to overcome me. I paused for a second to let it pass through. "I promised her that we would. But it turns out it is illegal in the state of Tennessee. This is the alternative that we came up with."

Lifting my glass, I said, "For, Rita."

"For Rita," everyone echoed.

I turned on the projector and images appeared of thousands of Chinese lanterns being released over a lake. The effect of it with the backdrop of luminaires we'd placed along the street and on the tables, left us awestruck.

We watched silently, honoring the life of Rita Winston.

I hoped that from wherever she was, that she could see this and feel all the love pouring out for her.

Molly laced fingers together with mine before lifting my hand to her lips. It was so natural between us, as though we'd always known each other.

I closed my eyes and listened for the mournful cry of the whippoorwill, but tonight it remained elusive. And I eventually, gave up trying.

EPILOGUE

Time rolled on with incredible speed.

There were many times when I'd pause within its folds and marvel at the steps I'd taken to get to that point. I'd think about how my decisions had shaped everything, how miraculous everything had become after I'd found the right path, and how I could have never, in a million years, guessed that I would be as fortunate as I was.

Then in the next moment, Hal junior would send a golf ball through the kitchen window, nearly taking my eye out, and it would bring me back fully into the present, back into the duties of being a good husband, a good father, and a good therapist.

I'd race out to find him hiding in the treehouse that we had built together, almost exactly like the one I'd used to take refuge from my mother's unchecked emotions.

Then I'd lecture him about using his brain because that was what it was made for. I'd make him help me clean up the mess and then I would let it go and forgive him, because we all made mistakes.

When I had asked Molly if our Hal looked the same as the child whom she had seen all those years ago, climbing into bed with my mother, she had said, "You know it's funny. I can't remember his face anymore."

"Why do you think that is?" I had asked.

She'd shrugged. "It was only a prelude of possible things to come. It wasn't fully formed then, so it slipped away, kind of like a dream would."

Because of Molly's uncertainty over identity, I hadn't really grounded Hal at birth.

Then Joseph was born.

We moved into a bigger house on a 13-acre lot, surrounded by farm land and a lake.

I discovered that I possessed a green thumb and gardening became another outlet to pour myself into. My cornstalks grew so tall that I was afraid the children would climb them and inadvertently bring back a giant.

Rita came next, our first girl, and lastly Caroline, two years later, both the splitting image of Molly.

As our children began to fill our lives with equal parts joy and headaches. Molly and I decided that the pace of the outside world would not rule us and that we would always make our decisions based strictly around our love for each other and what was best for the family as a whole.

And I believe we succeeded, although it was not our intention, to eventually bring up individuals who were strong in their own right, not easily swayed by outside opinions, with strong moral compasses.

They grew to seek answers not from others, but from the divine voice inside of themselves.

When the children demanded details about my mother, I showed them the small sampling of photographs that I had. There was one of Rita as a little girl, looking demure in patent leather dress shoes and lacey, white, ankle socks, and of her smirking as only a teenager could, astride a grey and black horse.

Their favorite of Rita, was one that I had taken of her with a polaroid camera bought with grass cutting money. She was seated on the couch, likely with her first vodka and coke of the evening, staring off into the distance.

She'd looked almost dreamy, as if she had suddenly pulled a memory out of the ether that was happy. I'd wanted to capture it so that I could later dissect it, and maybe in doing so, discover its origin.

I tried to be truthful with them about my experiences because this was something that had always been missing in my earlier life. I gave them all of those details that allowed me to make sense to them.

Sometimes their eyes would grow wide with disbelief, or they would laugh about something that was so over the top, it could almost pass for dark comedy.

I even told them about the time that I was a smartassed teenager and my mother had put me out of the car in the middle of nowhere. I had eventually found my way home in the dark, a bit shaky, but otherwise, unharmed.

But I also talked a lot about the way she was in the end, the grace that came into her right before she died. I tried to paint a picture of what she must have been like when she met my father, when she was happy and completely enamored with the life that she thought she was going to have.

I had help from the Chandley family in filling in details about my father. They had given me a box of pictures that Molly organized into albums. From these relatives we gained stories about Joseph that helped us incorporate him into our world.

I told the kids about how I grew up not knowing anything about him, and that before I even knew he existed, he had haunted their mother.

This always made them smile.

There wasn't a day that went by that I didn't look over at Molly doing something completely ordinary, like putting a band-aid on skinned knee, or reading a book, and think, *wow, I really won the lotto.*

Or one of the kids would say something so profound and unexpected that I would think, *did this child really come from my DNA?*

There also wasn't a day that went by that I wasn't thankful for all that I had in my life. I was grateful—for every heartache, every blessing, every golf ball through the window.

I'd done a pretty good job of training myself to see the bigger picture, the miracles within the things that didn't look like miracles at all. But they were always there, even within the thick of the hardest things, curled up within our deepest illusions and limiting beliefs, waiting for us to notice them.

I could fill an entire book with the off the wall things Molly had said over the years. Sometimes they were full of so much wisdom, it took days to unravel it. A favorite of mine, be better not bitter, was simple enough.

We shouldn't waste time dwelling on the mistakes of the past and the things that hurt us. The past no longer exists. To cling to it, means to destroy all the potential within the present, and delay the blessings of the future.

My world was not composed of perfection. It was not easy. It was challenging, even grueling at times. But I never begrudged the hard times, because even those brought me closer to God, closer to my true nature and my reason for existing.

The bubble had been the hardest gift to understand. I was taken to my knees, humbled, and my ego stripped from me. I was forced to sit with my pain and to look into its face.

I had to do that.

Without that time, I would have never been able to release it. I wouldn't have begun to live. I would have just kept hiding.

And if I knew that tomorrow, I would have to go back in time and go through the same experiences all over again. I don't think I *would* pack up my bags and drive my car over a cliff, or throw in the towel.

Instead, I would brush myself off and lean into the wind. And I would be excited about getting another chance to experience all of my days, all the small miracles, moonlight kisses with Molly, first steps, bonfires in pajamas, and all of the weirdness of the world I'd created with the people I adored most in it.

The End